LOVE 'EM OR
LEAVE 'EM

LOVE 'EM OR LEAVE 'EM

•

Angie Stanton

Montlake
Romance

Text copyright ©2010 by Angela Tyler
Printed in the United States of America.

Published by Montlake Romance
P.O. Box 400818
Las Vegas, NV 89140

ISBN-13: 9781477814475
ISBN-10: 1477814477

This is for you, Mom.
I miss you dearly.

Special thanks to my amazing screwball family, Ed, Kristi, and Kevin. You make my days worth living. This book wouldn't have been possible without my incredible critique group and the extraordinary women of WisRWA Madison.

Thanks to my numerous girlfriends; you make life so much fun and are always willing to kick me in the butt when I'm down. A special call out to the women from "Not the Book Club Club," who will never see this, because they don't like to read.

This story could not have been written without the reality television genre. You make a girl wonder, What if it were me? And finally I thank all the good-looking quarterbacks in the NFL who make women want to watch football.

Chapter One

Ashley tried to pinpoint exactly how she'd gotten into this mess. As the limo cruised past the palatial estates along the beaches of Southern California, she flipped open her phone and hit Redial. Within seconds, a voice came on the line.

"You can't call me now. You're not even supposed to have a phone."

"Kelli, what on earth was I thinking? How did I let you talk me into this?" Kelli, her trusted friend, knew her most embarrassing moments and deepest secrets.

"Where are you, Ashley? Tell me exactly."

"You know I would do anything for you, but this goes beyond the limits of friendship." Decked out in a black silk designer gown she'd never seen before tonight, Ashley sat with the phone to her ear. The cutest shoes adorned her feet. Thin black straps crisscrossed daintily over her feet and tiny rhinestones sparkled like diamonds.

"Ashley?"

"I'm in the car—I mean, the limo. We're driving by big houses. I might throw up." She was moments away from her appearance in the latest version of a television reality dating show titled "Love 'Em or Leave 'Em." "I hate these shows."

"I know, but you're doing me the biggest favor in the world. I owe you big-time. Think chocolate martinis."

She was saving Kelli's job. At the last moment, one of the contestants had arrived at the pre-show meeting with a full-blown case of chicken pox. Makeup covered the girl's face so thick it could be scraped off with a butter knife. The pock-faced girl had begged the producers to allow her to stay on, but with no success. So Kelli had pleaded with Ashley to save both the day and Kelli's job as casting director.

Ashley leaned back and tried to relax. She stared through the tinted sunroof at the night sky as she spoke into the phone. "What am I doing? Yesterday I was searching the want ads for a new job. Today I'm with a group of young single bimbos fighting for the hand of some desperate bachelor who probably only wants a quick tumble, or his fifteen minutes of fame."

"Get ahold of yourself. You can do this. Remember the plan? All you have to do is behave yourself, keep under the radar—"

"And I'll be off this stupid show tonight. You know this goes against everything I believe in. Since when did it become okay to go on a television game show to decide the rest of your life? To fall in love in six short weeks during sweeps to keep America entertained? It isn't right. Who possibly believes these shows are reality?"

Ashley knew, from all the pre-planning Kelli did for the network, that they planned these farces down to the last detail so they would come off without a glitch. Each girl was chosen for the harem of airheaded Barbie dolls for a specific reason.

"I understand how you feel. Hang in there, and if everything goes as planned, you'll be off the show tonight."

"I hate this."

"I know, and I'm sorry. If I knew of any other way, I would have taken it. You're my last resort and I'm eternally grateful. Now listen up. I want you to pull yourself together. You look great and you're going to be fine."

Ashley glanced down at her quickly polished self. Kelli had steamrolled her to get ready in time. "I'm going to call you again later so I can whine and you can grovel some more."

"No you're not. Now tuck the phone away, and don't let anyone know you have it. Take a few deep breaths and enjoy the moment. You look great! Try to enjoy yourself."

"Not likely. I'll see you tomorrow. At least I'd better. Enjoy my suffering and pain, because this will never happen again." She flipped the phone shut and slipped it into her tiny handbag, took her prescribed breaths, and glanced back down at her feet.

Her toes looked majorly good, thanks to a pedicure the week before. A makeup artist had crafted a masterpiece on her normally plain, girl-next-door looks. Her medium-blond hair, however, could have used more time. She viewed herself as more of a casual girl. Never much makeup. Her at-home attire was usually a long T-shirt and loose shorts with her favorite pair of comfortable orange flip-flops. Definitely not classy.

The limo slowed and turned onto a long, brick-paved drive ending in a large circular area in front of a beautiful mansion. The whole scene was right out of a magazine spread depicting a Spanish countryside villa. *Oh geez.* Cameras were everywhere. How could she have forgotten the cameras? She hated this even more. *Please let me survive this and get out with my sanity intact, if not my pride.* Ashley would rather slide through life unaware and alone than flaunt herself in front of the cameras looking like a desperate debutante. *Please let this be painless and as short as possible.*

The limo rolled to a stop between two large light stands. Tripods held three cameras and two more were handheld. A few feet from her door a large figure loomed.

Oh no, there he is.

He was tall, over six feet, and broad across the

shoulders. His posture commanded attention as he waited, one hand casually in his pocket. He appeared lean and fit, with narrow hips and long, lanky legs. Her heart rate increased as she took in his confident stance. She couldn't see his face, but he seemed attractive in shadow.

Okay, this might not be half bad. Hanging out with some hot guy would certainly soften the blow. There were a lot worse ways to spend her time.

Ashley wondered who he was. All Kelli would say was that he was well-known and liked by everyone.

There was a certain kind of guy Ashley preferred, and her type most certainly wouldn't be the kind to put himself on television to find a date.

She perched nervously on the edge of the leather seat, palms sweaty and heart racing. Her queasy stomach emitted a loud rumble, objecting to the stress. She battled the impulse to lose her cookies then and there.

The door opened and bright lights blinded her.

Time froze.

She sat unmoving. They waited for her. She couldn't do it. She took a deep breath and let it out slowly, trying to convince herself to get out of the limo. It wouldn't be so bad. She was a strong woman, and had survived more difficult times than this.

With a steely grip on the door and a forced smile on her lips, she cautiously stepped out of the car and moved forward to meet the mystery man. The cameras surrounded her. Bright lights beat down on her. Blinded her.

Toto, we are not in Kansas anymore.

As she stepped forward, the shadow of the man became visible behind the glare. She continued toward him with what she hoped was a friendly smile for the camera.

Wham!

Fabric ripped as she was propelled toward the concrete by the speed of her own momentum. Out of the corner of her eye, Ashley saw Mister Broad Shoulders lunge forward, but she was too fast. It was "Bachelorette Eats Sidewalk." *Unbelievable!* She wanted to fly under the radar, not hit it straight on, like a bug on a windshield.

She sprawled on the sidewalk as though she had just slid into home plate headfirst. Her hands stung like mad, and her knee hurt like heck.

Pretty sure I just tore the borrowed dress.

Two large feet shod in well-polished shoes stood before her.

How could she graciously exit this scene? Could you say "take two" in reality TV? Maybe she should crawl back into the limo before it pulled away and never come back.

Ashley wished the sidewalk would open up and swallow her whole. She grit her teeth in humiliation. Feeling like a total fool was nothing new. She had a knack for finding embarrassing situations.

Crawling to her hands and knees in an unladylike fashion, Ashley felt warm hands on her shoulder and arm as the mystery man attempted to help her up.

She glanced around and prayed for someone to yell "Cut," or step forward and say "Let's try it again," but no one did.

A deep, husky voice said, "Let me help you." There was a hint of a Southern accent and a concerned tone in his voice.

"No, I'm fine." Lifting her dress out of the way, Ashley tried unsuccessfully to pull away from his gentle grip.

As she stood, her eyes scanned the man in front of her from toes up. *Dang, he was tall.*

She pushed the hair out of her face and looked at his hands, still resting reassuringly on her bare skin. Ashley tilted her head up toward the low voice and repeated, "I'm fine."

His eyes showed sincere concern. She quickly glanced away, not ready to connect with him. This was not the stunning entrance she'd hoped for her television debut, but it was memorable nonetheless.

And then he had the nerve to laugh at her. Okay, not laugh, but definitely chuckle. Ashley faced him with strands of mussed hair stuck to her lip gloss. She pushed the hair away from her mouth and felt lines of gloss streak across her cheek.

He held her shoulder to keep her steady and looked at her no-longer-perfectly-made-up face. With an arched eyebrow, he grinned a devilish smile. "Falling for me already?"

Their eyes connected.

Zzzt. Her body went numb.

Hunky NFL quarterback Luke Townsend stood before her. The icon of football, complete with his trademark chiseled jawline and a day's beard growth. Why would a big shot like him be on a reality dating show? Who cared?

Ashley stared up at him, her jaw wide open. *Great. He can see my fillings.*

He smiled and laughed at her obvious awe of him.

Ashley nervously laughed back and then noticed the producers waving her toward the entrance to the mansion. She numbly walked past him into the building, looking back every few steps to make sure it was really him.

I have just fallen at the feet of Luke Townsend. He was the quarterback for the Green Bay Packers, the team revered by everyone from Wisconsin and beyond. *The gods are laughing at me now. I know they are.* Everyone she knew and everyone they knew would watch this show. There were no more loyal fans in the world than Packer fans. *I think I'm going to curl up and die right at this moment. Yup, I think it would be the best way to go.*

Inside the mansion more cameras lurked, and the crowd of gorgeous young women grew, each woman more beautiful than the next. Ashley knew one thing for sure: she did not belong in this crowd.

She approached the mass of decked-out ladies and found, instead of a vicious pack of women sizing each other up, a sorority party. Certainly they checked out the competition, but all claws were sheathed for the moment.

"Did you see him?" exclaimed a tall blond bombshell with an unnaturally large bosom.

A curvaceous brunet with perfect teeth squealed, "He is totally gorgeous!"

"Did you know he was a football player?" asked a platinum blond with a dress cut down to her pierced belly button.

Ashley maneuvered through the group in hopes of finding a quiet corner.

Another long-limbed beauty exclaimed, "What's his name? Where's he from? I've never heard of him, but who cares!"

Ashley hung to the side as the room filled with more stunning women. Most didn't know who Luke Townsend was, which proved they weren't watching football on Sunday afternoons.

The women all resembled Miss America or America's next supermodel. Ashley was more like the girl with a bad haircut. She didn't mind, though. She felt pretty normal, and it was fine with her. *I won't be threatening any of the bathing beauties here.*

The questions and chatter continued until the

twenty-fifth and final "bachelorette" entered the mansion. Then, on cue, in walked the host, Clay Stevens. Clay looked like a nobody trying to make it in Hollywood via another reality television show. His reddish blond hair spiked out all over his head like a Ryan Seacrest wannabe. It didn't go well with his black tuxedo, which hung limply over his shoulders.

"Welcome to the Seville Mansion, ladies," he said in his fake Hollywood voice. "I'm sure you're anxious to know more about our bachelor, so I won't make you wait any longer. Ladies, may I introduce NFL quarterback Mr. Luke Townsend." Clay stepped aside, extending his arm toward the door.

Luke wore an easygoing smile as he walked through the foyer and down the steps into the great room. He towered above all the women in their stiletto heels.

"Good evening, ladies," he said. "It's a pleasure to finally meet you all." He smiled and nodded tentatively as he gazed around the room.

Ashley knew each woman hoped to receive one of his fifteen cherished roses at the end of the night.

"I must say, I don't think I've ever been surrounded by such ravishing beauties before in my life."

Much preening and eye fluttering followed. There were many hellos and nervous smiles. Some girls, more brazen than others, walked up to reintroduce themselves after their brief meeting outside the limos. A few took his hand and petted it as they talked, or brushed against him to make sure he was aware of them.

Ashley did not want to be remembered. Her plan was to be an unnoticed mouse in the corner and go home. Tonight. She had no intention of being subjected to any more "spontaneous reality TV."

Annoying host Clay instructed everyone to find a seat or stand around the edge of the room as Luke greeted the beauty queens, hand petters, and gold diggers.

"I must say, I feel a little nervous with so many of you and only one of me." Luke surveyed the packed room. "As you know, I'm not used to so much attention."

Hoots and screams of joy erupted. He glanced around, his bright blue eyes scanning everyone. Most of the women leaned forward to get the best view and to make eye contact as often as possible. A statuesque brunet in a red satin dress sat across from Luke directly in his line of vision. Poised on the edge of her seat with the slit of her dress open, she revealed long slender legs crossed alluringly, which often drew his eyes.

Ashley sat at the back of the group on the edge of the tile fireplace. Arms crossed, she avoided eye contact with Luke as she observed the behavior of the others.

A gorgeous blond perched on the back of the sofa hung on his every word. She looked like a model right off the cover of *Cosmo* in her silky gold, formfitting gown. It was cut low, revealing more than a decent woman should. A rail-thin woman with a porcelain complexion and a brilliant blue dress sat twirling the ends of her silky black hair. She eyed Luke with blatant desire.

"I was born and raised in Whiskey Bayou, Louisiana, along with a brother and a sister," he said, moving around the room. "I've devoted my entire life to football and now find myself fast approaching the end of the road. At least as far as my athletic career goes."

Eager faces bobbed up and down like little dogs sitting in the back of a car window, agreeing with his every word.

"As you can guess, all the time I spent on and around the football field really didn't leave me with much time to pursue a serious relationship." Ashley heard an excited intake of breath around the room. "So, here I am at thirty-two, and heck, my clock is ticking."

There was more twittering from the peanut gallery.

"So when this opportunity came up to meet so many eligible and lovely women, I figured, why not." He stood. "I'm hoping to meet the woman of my dreams and finally settle down. In fact, it would be a perfect end to what has turned out to be a perfect career for me."

Ashley saw many ambitious eyes glitter at the prospect of being the woman of his dreams. She didn't want to be anywhere near his dreams.

"I look forward to getting to know each one of you in the days and weeks ahead." He glanced at everyone and then over to Clay. "So let's get this party started!"

Music pumped through the room where women stood in clusters. Only a few at a time could huddle around Luke so it was easy for Ashley to stay clear. Some of the women really worked him, while others played games, acting shy or coy. It was entertaining to see how each woman tried to win and then keep his attention.

Meanwhile, the food and drink flowed. Although it was a big party atmosphere, Ashley met a couple of very nice girls. Liz, a tall beautiful brunet with long flowing hair and almond-shaped eyes, seemed real and was easy to talk to—in spite of her great looks. She was working on her master's thesis and hoped to take a couple of months to travel around Europe when she finished. Rachel had an earthy look. A petite five feet two inches with a short, light brown pixie cut, she carried herself with confidence. She told Ashley that appearing on the show was another great adventure. She had backpacked her way through Panama the previous year and planned to save up her cash to spend a year in New Zealand. *Now, hers is a life I want.* Apparently she had tried out for "Love 'Em or Leave 'Em" as a lark. She could never meet the right guy and thought it would be a lot of fun, and if she was lucky, maybe even net her a rich, good-looking hubby.

"So, what brings you here?" Liz asked. "You don't look like the kind trying to make it in Hollywood by appearing on a reality show."

"You've got that right." Ashley glanced around at all the probable model and actress wannabes and wondered how to answer without confessing the real story.

"I guess you could call it an impulse decision I made after losing my job and getting dumped." She took a deep breath, recalling the painful experience. "Or say that it was a weak moment when I saw the ad for the show and applied. It was a total rebound decision." She quickly added, "I thought if there's ever a chance to find a perfect match, this would be it."

Okay, so the getting-dumped part was true, but the perfect-match thing was total bull.

"So you're on the rebound," Rachel stated. "What a drag. Was it serious? The guy you were with?"

It was a sore spot Ashley didn't want to talk about. After dating exclusively for three years—at least *she'd* dated exclusively—it turned out that Ken was quite active on the side.

Ashley swallowed the painful memories. "Suffice it to say, he'd been cheating on me long enough to join a singles club."

"What a pig!" Rachel said.

At the moment, Ashley felt all men were pigs.

"You poor thing. But it was a definite blessing," Liz pointed out. "What if you'd married the creep? Best to be rid of him now."

Liz and Rachel sympathized with Ashley's bad luck in career and romance, and agreed that this was a great place for her to relax, burn off some steam, and date a cute hunk while she tried to figure out life. The only problem was she didn't want to date Luke or any other guy.

"So, what do you think of our bachelor?" asked Liz.

"Not too hard on the eyes, but a little on the tall side for my taste," responded Rachel.

"Not for me." Liz grinned. "He is the perfect size. I like my guys tall. It's nice to be able to look up at a guy instead of eye-to-eye. However, I wonder if this one has much of a brain. It's never a complete package, you know. If you get the looks, there's no brain."

"You can't have it all," Rachel remarked. "I just hope he has a sense of adventure."

"Are you kidding? Jocks are always full of adventure," replied Ashley. "They can't wait to climb the next mountain. I mean it literally. Guys like him are all about competition. They want to conquer the next challenge."

"What did he say to you when you met him outside?" asked Liz.

"He was actually very nice," Rachel said. "He introduced himself and welcomed me to the show."

"Ashley, what did you think when you met him?" Liz asked.

Not sure how to respond, she nibbled her lip before admitting, "I wanted to throw up."

Liz and Rachel laughed loudly, attracting attention from some of the other women.

"I'd love to see that," said Rachel. "What an opening." Trying to cover her reluctance to be on this show, Ashley said, truthfully, "I really hate cameras. And the idea that I'm supposed to open up to some total stranger in front of the entire country makes me nauseous." She gestured to the cameras with her arms. "Plus, I feel kind of like a piece of meat, as though we're new cars and this guy gets to test drive us all before picking one and driving it home." She leaned close and whispered, "Come on, don't you think it's a little bit creepy?"

"True." Rachel smiled. "But, hey, a test drive could be kind of fun." Her eyebrows lifted in a playful manner. "Plus, you don't have to take the rose if he offers you one."

"Oh, yes you do," interrupted Liz. "Didn't you listen at the contestant meeting? The show is leaving it all up to the bachelor. You can't bail out early even if you want to. It's all in your contract. Anyway, who in their right mind would want to bail out? This is going to be an absolute riot. I definitely want a rose. I want to see how this whole thing unwinds, and who he picks, and who he doesn't. It's a great study of human psychology."

"So, what did he say when you met him?" Rachel asked again.

Groaning, Ashley responded reluctantly. " 'Are you okay?' "

"What? He asked, 'Are you okay?' " Liz was confused.

"You didn't actually throw up on him, did you?" teased Rachel.

"No, I pretty much wiped out at his feet. It was quite a grand entrance. How many of the women here tonight can say they took a nosedive in front of the guy they're supposed to impress?" Her face warmed with embarrassment as she retold the story.

"See, I even ripped the bottom of my dress." Ashley lifted her dress to show the torn hemline. "Do either of you have scissors? With my luck, the next time I take a step I'll get caught in this and take out half the room."

"Unbelievable! You actually fell down in front of him! You are too much." Rachel giggled and Liz joined right in. She couldn't hold back. Ashley started to laugh too.

"That's not even the worst of it," Ashley added. "I ruined a perfect pedicure!" She again lifted the torn dress high enough for them to see the gouged toenail and chipped polish.

Their friendship solidified over more stories of life's embarrassing moments. But Ashley was the only one unfortunate enough to have hers caught on film.

As the evening wore on, the producers made sure each contestant met and talked alone with Luke for a few minutes, before the first fateful rose ceremony. Ashley desperately hoped he wouldn't remember her.

"Ashley?" A tall, skinny producer called across the room.

"Yes?"

"You're next."

She set down her drink and joined him.

"This way, please."

The moment she had dreaded arrived. The producer directed her out of the main room down a wide, tiled hallway and around a corner. Her heart raced and she could barely breathe. She tried to calm herself. *How hard can it be? I'll just be sure to make this bad enough that he won't want to keep me, yet not so bad that I'll humiliate myself on national TV.*

A comfortable rattan love seat was positioned in an open-air summer room, directly before a low, open window that showcased a spectacular view of San Diego in the distance. Twinkle lights hung from the trees in the garden area and the scent of lush flowering trees and shrubs drifted everywhere.

Two cameras hovered above at different angles, one on Luke and one on the empty seat beside him. Microphone booms and lights also crowded the area. Ashley's stomach cramped in anxiety as she stepped over the cables to meet the football legend.

"Hello again." He reached for her hand as he stood to greet her. With heels on, she only needed to look up a few inches.

Unexpectedly tongue-tied and starstruck, she opened her mouth to say "Hi," but instead out came a jumble of nonsense. This time she stumbled over her tongue, not her dress. She looked up at him in desperation.

Luke was quick to put her at ease. "Should I brace myself in case you try to tackle?"

She tried to think of a way to steer the topic to something forgettable and uninteresting.

"You know I'm Luke, but somehow I didn't catch your name when you made your entrance earlier." He leaned forward as though he couldn't wait to hear what she might say.

Determined to overcome her nervousness, she responded, "That's because I didn't toss it out!" Immediately she laughed. "Get it? It's a quarterback joke! 'Didn't toss it out.' " Her nervous laugher turned into a snort. *Oops.*

Luke looked at her oddly, as though not quite sure what was going on.

Did he think she'd fallen at his feet on purpose to get his attention? She hoped not.

Smiling nervously as the joke tanked and knowing the cameras were on close-ups, she looked at him cautiously, unsure how to proceed. She cleared her throat and tried again. "I'm Ashley Reynolds." She paused. "Like the wrap."

His face scrunched in confusion.

"You know, like Reynolds Wrap." *Please, someone shut me up!*

"Nice to meet you, Ashley Reynolds," Luke said cautiously, as though she'd truly lost a gasket. Nonetheless, he took her hand with his large powerful one that had won Super Bowls and looked into her eyes as though he wanted to imprint her in his mind for later.

"Where are you from?" he asked.

"Wisconsin."

"No kidding." He smiled. "We're practically neighbors, then. Where in Wisconsin?"

"Madison, so I wouldn't say we're neighbors."

"Okay, so then you must know all about the Packers." He leaned back comfortably in the seat with his arm stretched behind her.

She nodded. It wasn't possible to grow up in Wisconsin and not know about the team or its huge following. Articles ran in the newspapers and on the news every night from the national draft to each practice. Mostly the news was about Luke. He was the darling of the team, young and good-looking, with way too much confidence and attitude.

"Have you ever been to a game?" His blue eyes sparkled as he talked about his team.

"As a matter of fact, I have," she replied, a smile growing on her face as she thought back.

"Did you enjoy it?"

"Yes and no. It was about three years ago on an ungodly hot fall day."

"Yes," he said, watching her with interest.

"Some friends of mine and I joined a bus tour. Not a pretty sight," she said, shaking her head. "We partied all the way from Madison, and then tailgated until we almost missed kickoff. Probably not what you wanted to hear."

"No, go on," he encouraged.

"I'm pretty sure we enjoyed the game. However, I honestly don't recall much other than the fact we did the Wave and danced every time there was a touchdown. You must have played a good game," she said, trying to look convincing, "because I know we danced a lot."

Not wanting to feed his already overinflated ego, she added, "But I'm really a Cowboys fan, which is why I went to the game. Tony Romo is hot. Wow!" She pretended to fan herself from the instant flush at the mention of the Wisconsin-raised quarterback.

"The Cowboys?" he asked in disbelief. "You need to get a life."

"But the tailgating was amazing," she said to bring the discussion back around. "I've never had so much fun before."

"It sounds pretty typical." He nodded in understanding. "My brother is always telling me about it. The stories are legendary. I see a lot of it getting started when I arrive hours before game time. Some days I feel like jumping the fence and joining in, but I have a job to do. Still, it's a lot of fun watching the fans bring in grills, loads of food, banners, and sometimes even live bands to play in the parking lot." He leaned back and crossed one leg over the other at the ankles. Masculine energy radiated off of him.

"Sometimes I think the tailgating is more fun for the fans than the actual game."

"No other fans tailgate like Packer fans," he commented. "Some party, but Packer fans have a lot of serious traditions going on."

"They have to do something to keep warm."

"I'm glad you had a good time, even if you don't remember me or the game." His eyebrows raised as he regarded her. "I don't remember you either," he teased.

Ashley soaked in his essence. He was larger than life in demeanor and physical stature. Tall, broad, and muscular, he commanded a room as he commanded his team. And yet, he had the perfect boy-next-door face, including the faded scar on his upper lip. Put the whole picture together, and wow! He was fine looking! Over the years, she'd seen dozens of pictures of him in the paper, but he was much better looking in the flesh. Tonight he looked great in the dark jacket and turtleneck. Maybe it would be okay if she hung around for a little longer, just to enjoy the eye candy.

The producer signaled that time was up. Ashley stood. "It's been a pleasure meeting you and finally putting a real person with all those news photos," she said.

"I'll look forward to seeing you later, Madison." And off she went, confused, wondering what he meant. Luke had made it sound like he would see her later. Did he mean he would be keeping her around? She hoped not . . . sort of. As she rounded the corner to rejoin the party, she felt glad she'd had the chance to actually sit down and talk with the famous Luke Townsend. He seemed like a nice normal guy.

And he was a hottie.

Chapter Two

Never had Ashley seen such a display of powdered and glossed perfection. She couldn't believe how beautiful the women were. Each wore an elegant long evening dress fit for the Oscars. The picture the room made with all the gorgeous flowers and women should have been on the cover of *Vogue*.

Producers, cameras, and lighting crew filled the great room, along with a variety of miscellaneous assistants who moved about. Furniture was pushed out of the way. The producers carefully placed the twenty-five contestants so each could be seen by one of the numerous cameras looming in the room. Luke stood on the other side of the room facing the women, a basket of long-stem red roses sitting on a table beside him. The excitement and tension in the room grew by the minute.

A middle-aged man stepped up to the front and introduced himself. "Hello, may I have everyone's attention please?" The room quieted immediately with anticipation.

"I'm Jim Davis, the senior producer of the show. I'd like to officially welcome you as we kick off what we hope becomes the first in a long line of 'Love 'Em or Leave 'Em' seasons.

"First, let's quickly review a couple of items. Cameras will be a part of everything. Expect to see them everywhere you go and catching everything you do." The women exchanged both nervous and excited looks at the mention of the voyeuristic cameras. "The only place they will not be allowed is in the bathrooms. I know it feels intrusive, but in a day or so, you will barely notice them."

My eye. Ashley looked around the room filled with bright lights, power cables, cameramen, and producers. The last thing she could imagine was getting used to them.

"Our cameramen are all professionals. Their job is to catch the fun and exciting moments, and to be as unobtrusive as possible. However"—he stopped pacing and faced them directly—"they are *not* allowed to speak to you and you are not allowed to speak to them. If you have any problems or concerns, please see me or one of the assistant producers, but only if absolutely necessary. We want to leave you on your own to interact and make this experience as natural as possible."

"Finally, I'd like to remind you of the contracts you signed. You committed to participate willingly in the show until the leading man releases you. We have wonderful tape of all your entrances. Congratulations on a great start. Now, the show is in your hands so relax, have fun, and be yourselves."

Too many experiences in Ashley's life were caught on film. Most turned out to be embarrassing and painful.

Back in high school she'd become the target of a school prank. Tom Hanson was the dreamiest guy Ashley had ever laid eyes on. Her crush on him consumed her. Unfortunately, it annoyed Tom. Once he discovered her open worship, it became his life's mission to humiliate her. As the photographer for the school newspaper, his camera became a weapon of mass embarrassment. Her adoration had turned into humiliation when he'd put her picture in the school paper with the caption *Most in need of a makeover*.

That had only been the beginning. Terrible pictures of her popped up everywhere. When she tried on costumes for the school play, he caught her unaware and captured horror on her face as she stood in her 32AA bra and "Tuesday" underwear, on a Monday. He took photos of her wiping her nose, and the time she walked out of the girls' bathroom with toilet paper stuck to her shoe. Whenever she did something stupid, which was often, he caught it on film. The jerk ran off copies of her bad underwear shots and put them up all over the school. She became pin-up material in many of the boys' lockers. There was no way to stop it. He even slipped slides of her into a science class slide show. After that experience, it had become her life's mission to avoid cameras, not to mention letting a guy know when you felt something for him.

So far she'd already embarrassed herself when she'd tripped on her dress. Thank goodness she hadn't chipped a tooth. It made her more determined than ever to avoid the cameras as much as possible. She would stay under the radar. With so many women, it shouldn't be too difficult. She'd just live in the bathroom all day.

It seemed like they had stood in formation for hours, doing nothing. Ashley's feet were killing her.

Now, with the pep talk over, the producers were ready to roll. Bright TV lights around the room glared, and the host, Clay Stevens, made his big entrance. He sauntered into the room with a pseudoserious expression, as though about to do rocket science instead of working a game show.

"Ladies, I trust you all enjoyed your opportunity to talk privately with Luke for a few minutes and make your best impressions," he said in his I'm-a-serious-journalist voice. "Luke, are you ready?"

Luke nodded, giving Clay the once-over. He couldn't seem to take his eyes from Clay's spiked and high-lighted hair. It stood straight up from all the product. He probably hired a highly paid person just to do his hair. What a waste of money.

"You may now begin the rose ceremony."

The electricity-charged atmosphere intensified. The air thickened with anticipation as each woman put on her game face. Some stood with overconfident looks while others gave pleading looks, as though sad, begging eyes would win his favor.

"Pk . . . pk . . . pk . . ."

What on earth was that noise? Ashley glanced to her left, sure she'd see a camera with one of its gizmos whirring.

The woman beside her stood, fists clenched, her features stretched into a mask of frightening intensity, muttering "Pick me, pick me, pick me . . ."

A brassy blond from the first row whipped her head around, smile dissolving into a snarl. "Shush." Her smile returned and she notched it to dazzling as she faced forward.

Ashley reached over and took the nervous woman's fist in her hand. "It's okay," she whispered. The tight knot of fingers relaxed a little.

Ashley tried to focus on the stucco wall behind Luke's head and look as uninvolved as possible without calling attention to herself. If she could make herself unnoticeable, he wouldn't pick her. It was like sitting right next to the teacher at school. If they couldn't easily see you, they would never call on you.

She really wanted off, but her promise to Kelli dictated she stay.

And so it began. Luke announced names one by one. Each time the woman he named stepped forward, he asked her if she would accept the rose. Of course, each said yes. Lindsey, Kate, Jenny . . . The names kept going. Then he said Rachel and Liz. It made her happy to see her two new friends make the cut. She could only think, *I'll finally be able to get out of these toe-crunching shoes soon.*

Gwen, the "pick me" girl, Melissa, Meg . . . As Luke got down to the last three roses he took more time. Perhaps he couldn't remember everyone's names, or maybe he just didn't know who to pick.

The remaining women tried not to look desperate while the cameras rolled and perspiration collected on their faces. While these women wished to stay in, Ashley prayed to get out. Almost there, almost free. Just a couple more roses and she could begin putting her life together again and try to figure out how to make Kelli pay her back for this one.

The ceremony dragged on forever as the producer kept stopping and starting to get different angles and correct the lighting. Ashley was exhausted. Her eyelids drifted shut. Sleep deprivation was not good for her. She began to daydream, that or sleep standing up. *Only a few more names.*

"Ashley."

Everyone looked at her. Rachel and Liz waved their hands in an attempt to get her attention. One edge of Luke's mouth tilted up as he eyed her across the room.

He repeated her name, but this time as a question, "Ashley?"

Ashley stood frozen. Panic rushed through her veins.

Luke stared. His eyebrows scrunched together.

"Oh geez, I'm sorry," she said as she stepped forward, embarrassed.

"No problem. You don't have to take it if you don't want to," he teased as he held the rose out of her reach.

Ashley replied with a big smile, "Okay," and began to turn away.

Before she turned even halfway, Luke reached out and took her arm for the second time that night and held her in place.

"Will you accept this rose?"

She paused, then shrugged. "Oh, why not?"

She took the rose from Luke's powerful hand and looked up to see him grinning, a mischievous twinkle in his eye. She couldn't help but grin back. Ashley stepped to the side with the other "winners." Liz and Rachel gave her the thumbs-up. They'd all made the first big cut from twenty-five down to fifteen.

Each of the "rejects" said good-bye to Luke on their way out. Then Clay brought out the champagne and everyone toasted the new adventure. Ashley found herself in great spirits after all. It had been an exhausting day and an interesting evening. Thankful she'd met two great women who would be joining her on the next leg of the show, she hoped they would also help buffer her from the insanity.

Bright morning light shone through the windows, mercilessly breaking through Ashley's exhausted sleep. No matter which way she rolled over or how she held the pillow over her head, the sun snuck through and annoyed her into wakefulness.

The background noise of distant squealing, shouting, and feet running past the door and down the stairs broke through her stupor. The cobwebs in her mind began to clear as she lay in bed somewhere between sleep and wakefulness. She was not at home in her own bed. She hadn't lost her job, and she didn't face eviction. She was in a huge house. No, a mansion, with strange women running around and squealing like ten-year-olds.

"Ashley, get up." Liz pounded on the door as she passed by.

Ashley flung the pillow off her head and opened her eyes. Along with the bright sunlight, it all came flooding back. She had slept in a mansion along with a bunch of women she didn't know. She was posing as an eligible woman who wanted desperately to land the bachelor, none other than hottie quarterback Luke Townsend.

No, no! She was trying to sneak her way off the show, take her quickie paycheck, and find a respectable job.

Ashley glanced around the room. Luckily, Liz and Rachel had tugged her along with them when rooms and roommates were picked, so she didn't have to feel alone. The fourth girl in the room was Gwen. Tired and overwhelmed by the time they found their room, Ashley had simply nodded hello and collapsed into bed, exhausted.

Looking around the small space, true reality began to sink in. During the rush for the best room, Ashley had stepped aside to avoid the stampede. The ones with views of the ocean or pool areas were taken quickly. This room was small. Four single beds filled it. Three had probably been added for the show. Two small dressers sat between the beds on each side. Terracotta-colored tile with bright Spanish-style hand-woven throw rugs covered the floor. There was a small desk in one corner and an oversized potted ficus tree in the other. A tiny excuse for a closet completed the space. The one redeeming quality was a small balcony holding two chairs and a tiny table. Off the side of the house opposite the pool area, the balcony's view mostly showed the driveway and parking circle, but also some palm trees and greenery. Very nice.

The door swung open and Rachel popped her head in. "Come on, you're missing it! The first mail arrived and there's a date tonight."

Ashley gave her a fake look of excitement. "Oh goody!"

"Hurry up," Rachel said, and disappeared.

Here we go, Ashley thought. She pulled herself out of bed and tried to put on her I'm-so-excited-to-be-here face.

Downstairs, chaos reigned. Bouncing, happy girls clad in little more than tank tops and panties filled the great room. With bronzed legs and long hair everywhere, it looked like a Victoria's Secret slumber party. Ashley glanced down at her pale, sun-starved skin and pulled her baggy T-shirt a little lower.

Tami, the tall brunet who'd worn the dress with the slit a mile high the night before, held the letter and waved it every few seconds. Her tiny midriff top exposed a pierced belly button and showed off its large ruby-colored stone. Tami's thick, dark mane had a gorgeous natural wave. It was hair to-die-for. Each time she raised the date letter in the air more shrieks erupted. The producer stood off to the side, yelling over the noise, "Wait until the cameras are in place." Finally, he gave the thumbs-up and Tami tore open the envelope and read the enclosed message out loud:

Good morning to all. I hope you slept well.
There's a full day ahead with many stories to tell.
Today I look forward to getting to know just a few.
For Jenny, for Shelby, and for Rachel too.
Now go grab your cameras. We're off to the zoo.

Screams again filled the room. A few moans and groans came from those left out, particularly Tami, who pouted as she handed off the note as soon as she saw her name wasn't on it.

Liz and Ashley rushed over to Rachel to bask in the glow of her excitement.

"Oh my gosh!" she cried. "I can't believe I'm on the first date. He likes me. This is unreal. Do you think he picked me?" She was flushed. "Do you think he likes me? He is so good-looking! What will I wear?"

They laughed at her nervousness. Last night Rachel had acted as though the whole thing didn't matter. She wanted to fund her next exotic trip, not win the man of the hour, and certainly not gush over some macho jock.

"Whatever you do, wear heels," Liz said, looking down at Rachel's petite five feet two inches. She patted her head. "He'll never see more than the top of your head if you don't."

"Don't worry, you'll look great whatever you wear," Ashley added. "You're the cutest thing in this room. You're gonna knock 'em dead."

"Great, you make me sound like a kitten, not a hot date," said Rachel, shaking her head.

Two hours later the lucky ladies waited for their date. Luke arrived in a sporty SUV limo. Dressed in khaki cargo shorts, a cream-colored golf shirt, and Tevas, he looked pretty amazing for a guy who wasn't trying. He smiled and waved at all the wallflowers as he opened the door for his dates. The three women fought for position while trying to act as if they were casually waiting for Luke.

One at a time, he took each by the hand and guided her into the limo. Rachel smiled demurely. Jenny went next. She didn't let him just take her hand—she walked right into his arms and gave him a squishy hug and what looked like a big wet smooch on the cheek. *Yuck.*

Shelby entered last and batted her baby blues as he took her hand. In her Southern drawl she crooned, "I just can't wait to get to know you a whole lot better, sugar." She leaned into him as she got in the limo and gave him a great view of her generously proportioned, store-bought bosom.

Luke wore a goofy smile as he climbed into the vehicle. It looked to Ashley like he thought, "Me too, honey, me too."

As the limo pulled away, the group left behind yelled good wishes and waved good-bye. Shelby leaned out the window and waved. "See you all later."

Standing there on the front steps of the mansion, the remaining twelve watched the limo drive down the manicured lane to the distant street. Ashley was relieved to see them go. The focus of the cameras would be elsewhere.

Liz and Ashley stood off to one side.

"Make good choices," yelled Ashley.

"No tongue kissing," hollered Liz. They giggled

and ducked down to avoid the camera as it panned across them.

The group headed back into the mansion.

"Thank God I didn't get picked," Tami announced. "There is no way I would traipse around a bunch of stinky animals in a zoo. I don't care how much money Luke makes."

"No kidding," chimed in Lindsey. "When he takes me out, it had better be in style. I didn't come here to be treated like a child. I expect linens and crystal, not popcorn and snow cones." She turned and walked back into the mansion.

"Look at Miss Hoity Toity," Ashley whispered to Liz. "You can see right up her nose, she's holding it so high." They walked back inside too, snickering as they went.

"Hello?"

"He gave me a rose."

"What?"

"Kelli. You said he wouldn't even notice me. That if I played it cool, I'd get right out and could go home." Ashley huddled on the toilet seat in the bathroom. The shower and sink ran full blast and the bathroom fan added to the noise.

"Are you serious? You're on the show! This is so exciting!"

"It is *not* exciting," she yelled in her whisper voice. "I did everything you asked. I put on the stupid dress and put myself through the ringer to get there in time.

I humiliated myself in front of the cameras and Lord knows how many other people." She stood and paced the small room. "I can't do this, Kelli. You know I can't. You said *'one day.'* You *promised*."

"Oh honey, I said 'probably one day.' There were no guarantees. Apparently he liked you. At least enough to get to know you more. It'll be fine."

"It will *not* be fine! I didn't bring enough underwear to stay longer! What am I supposed to do? I don't even know how this thing works." She swiped her hand across the steamed-up mirror. Her frustrated and frightened reflection stared back. "I'll look like an idiot next to all the other women. Have you seen these women? They're gorgeous. I'm not talking just pretty—I mean *incredible*." She turned her back on the face in the mirror and leaned against the sink.

"I know, Ashley. I helped select them. And stop selling yourself short. What are you doing on the phone? You know that's forbidden."

"Hey, I need a line to the outside world here. Kelli, I'm warning you, if this gig goes south on me, I am holding you responsible."

"Fine. Just remember, you can't let anyone know you don't want to be there. If the producers find out, I'll be fired. The rest of them all took personality tests, IQ tests, drug tests, and a bunch of other qualifiers. Now that you're staying for the next few days, I'd better fill up your file in case they go looking for backstory."

"Oh, Kelli, why did I let you get me into this?"

"Because you love me and would do anything for me."

"Yeah, yeah, I know. You creep. It is going to take a lot of chocolate for you to pay this one off."

"I'll have it ready and waiting the moment you get off the show. Heck, you may be free by this weekend."

"I'd better be! How am I going to survive in this mansion filled with love-starved beauty queens? They drive me nuts."

"You'll be fine. You always adapt well. Plus there are some very nice women there. I'm sure you'll make a friend or two."

"I suppose. I did meet two who are nice, but you should see some of them. One of them looks like she walked right out of a brothel. Oh, and another. Cricket! What is wrong with her parents? Who would name their kid 'Cricket'?"

"Her real name is Charlotte, and she's from a very nice family on the East Coast. Listen, I've got to run, but try to enjoy yourself. Who knows? You might even have fun."

Ashley flipped the phone shut. Fun. Sure. Then why did her stomach feel like it was sinking?

Ashley sat on her small bed, legs crossed. Rachel returned from the day at the zoo filled with information and ready to dish.

"Shelby, it turns out, is a genuine beauty-pageant girl." Rachel plopped on the edge of her bed.

"No big shocker there," Liz said.

"She came from a suburb of Dallas and grew up doing the beauty-contest circuit."

Ashley wasn't surprised. Shelby wore her blond hair long and highlighted to perfection. Her body was scary-amazing. Kind of like a Barbie look-alike.

"Her daddy's a plastic surgeon and he makes sure Shelby gets whatever she wants."

Liz and Ashley shared raised-eyebrow glances. Rachel continued, "Her perfect tiny nose was a sweet-sixteen gift."

It sure put Ashley's birthdays to shame. She celebrated hers with a cheap dinner out with her alcoholic dad and his latest flame. If she lucked out, the flame would be at least a few years older than Ashley. One year, the girlfriend brought Ashley a rose. She'd been one of the better ones. Of course, she was never seen again. When Ashley had turned twenty-one, she'd wised up and put contact with her father on an as-needed basis, which meant funerals and weddings.

"Oh, and then there's Jenny," Rachel added. "She played touchy-feely the whole time. She sat next to Luke every possible minute, and snuggled up to him as though he were her personal security blanket."

"Sounds like that girl has some attachment issues," Liz joked.

"No kidding. When we were at the zoo, she took his hand, pulled his arm over her shoulder, and hugged him as they walked."

"Were you able to get any time with him?" Ashley asked.

"Not much. It was like prying a dog off a bone to get near him. Between the beauty queen and the canine it wasn't easy." Rachel's eyes lit up. "But he did manage to get me alone in the sky-cab flight across the zoo."

"Now you're talking. Spill it, babe. What happened? Don't leave out anything." Liz leaned in to catch every detail.

"It was fun. He is so funny." Rachel grinned and covered her face with her hands, visibly shaking. "He said he felt like a rooster in a hen house with Jenny and Shelby around. And he said he wanted to get me alone to see if I had a voice, since all he'd heard so far were Shelby and Jenny."

A lovesick girl replaced the intelligent, independent young woman who had hiked across Central America. Ashley was surprised at the transformation.

"He is so handsome, and he's always aware of everyone around him. Even with the film crews and women positioning for his attention, he always spoke to all of us and kept us entertained."

More likely he is a womanizer and revels in all the attention. Why else would some good-looking rich guy agree to go on a show where he would be fought over and followed around by camera crews every minute? He was probably some exhibitionist who needed to be the center of attention.

"I'm glad you had such a great time." Ashley gave Rachel a big hug. It was nice to see her happy to be a part of the show.

One good thing Ashley learned: there was no shortage of competitive women wanting to win over Luke. Most likely, he would never get a minute alone without two or three bombshells surrounding him. It would give her every opportunity to keep her distance and fade into the background. With any luck, she wouldn't get a rose at the next ceremony and could collect her paycheck and go home.

"How's it hanging, bro?"

"Let me tell you, little brother. This is rougher than playing the Vikings at the dome."

"You jerk. You're swimming in gorgeous women and all you want to talk about is the Vikings?"

"Like I said, it's rough. Every time I turn around there's another one comin' at me. Some hit high, and some hit low. There're a lot of personal fouls going uncalled." Just talking to Mike made him feel better. There was nothing Luke liked more than to yank his brother's chain.

Luke heard Mike's wife in the background asking if he'd found anyone he liked yet. "Susan wants to know if you got lucky." Mike said.

"I did not!" Luke heard her yell back.

"Sounds like you're hating every minute of it too. So, 'fess up. Did you?"

"No, but there are a couple who are trying. It keeps the game interesting." He'd bet money he could land any one of them if he wanted to. That was the question. Did he want to? He'd spent the past seven years doing exactly that. His life was too shallow, too predictable. But on the other hand, it was simple, with no strings attached.

"You're so lucky. Why is it you always have all the fun while I'm left here to deal with the crap?"

"If I recall correctly, Mike, you're the one who cornered me into this deal." At first Luke had been angry about Mike's underhandedness. But after some consideration, he'd wondered if it might be a gift in disguise. If he wanted it to be, that is. Problem was, he wasn't sure what he wanted.

"Yes I did, and I'm proud of it. You can thank me later."

"It'll be a cold day."

"So, anyone promising? Any future wife-material?"

"Why is it you're always trying to get me married?"

"What can I say? Misery loves company."

Mike was the happiest man Luke knew. He and Susan had fallen in love as college students and were still going strong. They were quite a pair. They fought hard and loved hard. Always with laughter blended in.

"I've got enough misery thinking about how we lost in the playoffs."

"Come on, you lost the bet fair and square. Now you're obligated to give this the 'Luke Townsend try.'

If ever you've been in a situation to find the right woman, this could be it."

"Yeah, well, we'll see. I'm here—you should be glad."

"No complaints, man. I just want you to take advantage of the situation. The woman of your dreams could be in the group."

"I highly doubt there is a woman anywhere who could compete with my dreams. But I get the point. You and the family want me to settle down and act like a grown-up."

"Oh, you've got the grown-up part down, but you have definite issues in staying with a relationship."

Luke agreed, but relationships had never been his strong point.

"I've never found anyone worth staying loyal to. I keep telling you guys to give it time."

"Mom just worries about you staying single forever. She says you've been afraid of women ever since Crystal."

"Oh please, don't start that again," Luke said, rolling his eyes.

Early in his career, a beautiful woman had sucker punched him. He'd thought she was perfect. Instead she had turned out to be a conniving opportunist waiting to cash in on his sudden fame and fortune. He'd been ready to do the picket-fence thing, complete with a houseful of kids. Luckily, he'd figured her out in time. He'd lost fifteen thousand dollars on the ring and a whole lot of pride. Since then, trust and commitment needed to be earned.

"Tell Mom I'm fine and the only attachment issues I have are to ESPN and golf. And the last thing I am is lonely. Where there's one, there's seven, and the way they dress is enough to make a man go blind."

"You jerk."

"Sucks to be me—what can I say?"

"Anyone catching your attention?"

"There are a few interesting ones, but it's too early. Tell you what, you'll be the first to know. Hey, I've got to run. The car is here and I'm taking two beauties to the Padres game."

"Yeah, well, the space shuttle is here to fly me to the moon."

"Catch you later."

Chapter Three

How many bimbos does it take to sack a quarterback?

Luke was outnumbered and soon to be outmanned if he didn't watch his step. Jenny, the snuggler, was planted firmly at his hip. Wherever Luke went, Jenny followed, with puppy-dog eyes and clingy arms he couldn't seem to get away from. Several others surrounded the two of them, each of those women also vying for Luke's attention.

Ashley was seated with Rachel and Liz, watching the nuances of the game unfold from their lounge chairs a safe distance away, across the pool.

"Here comes trouble." Rachel pointed to the pool entrance.

Sure enough, Tami sauntered right into the thick of the harem.

"That woman has weapons and isn't afraid to use them," Ashley said.

Dressed in her skimpy black bathing suit and sheer cover-up, Tami prowled over to Luke in her spike-heeled sandals. They looked better suited for a fashion show than a pool party. Standing before him, she slowly slid her cover-up off her shoulders and tossed it directly at him.

"Want to take a dip?" she said in a low throaty voice. "I'm hot."

One corner of Luke's mouth tilted up. Without looking, he pushed the cover-up into Jenny's hands, his eyes remaining solely on Tami. He pulled off his T-shirt, stepped forward, and flung it over the girls' heads. It landed on an empty chair. He took Tami by the waist and led her to the deep end of the pool. After giving each other an I-know-what-you're-thinking grin, they dove into the clear, cool water of the pool.

So that's how the pros do it.

"Did you see that?" Liz asked sitting upright in her chair. "She is the reason women get no respect."

"Wow," Rachel exclaimed. "I never thought anyone could get him away from Jenny."

"I've never seen women act the way they do around him," added Ashley. "They're like a herd of lovesick cows."

"Thanks," said Rachel. "You think I'm a cow!"

Rachel's crush on Luke was getting more serious by the minute.

"No, not you. You weren't over there sniffing around him like the others. Just look at them. They look like they just lost their best friend. I think Gwen might actually cry."

Gwen was the fourth roommate in their tiny room, and she truly was mooning over Luke. Her pale blond hair reached down to her waist, and large cornflower blue eyes dominated her face. She looked like one of those paintings where the little girl's big eyes took up half her face, and always wore a pleading look. She desperately wanted Luke's attention, but so far hadn't gotten more than a cursory wave or casual smile in passing. Gwen just wasn't aggressive enough to play the game. Now she stood at the side of the circle of women as they all watched Tami and Luke frolic together in the water. Gwen seemed so disappointed, but obviously didn't have the nerve to jump in with them.

"How am I supposed to compete with that?" Rachel complained as Tami dove below the water, her shapely bottom popping out of the water as she went down. "She is the reason he never notices me!"

"You!" Ashley piped in. "At least you're cute, spunky, and tan. I feel like the ugly stepsister of the group."

"Oh please," Liz said. "You're beautiful in your own way."

"Ouch! That's hitting below the belt." Ashley cringed. "It's like the nice-personality thing." *I know I'm not drop-dead gorgeous, but I'm certainly not plain enough to have to rely only on my personality.*

"No," Rachel interrupted. "She means you're more like the girl next door. Right, Liz?"

"Exactly. You have natural beauty. Most of these girls are artificially beautiful. Their hair is processed, their skin has been bronzed, and they have implants. Heck, I wouldn't be surprised if most of them vomit to stay thin."

"Eww, please tell me you don't mean that," Ashley replied. "That is so wrong."

Horrified, she looked over at Rachel and Liz. "You don't make yourself vomit, do you?"

"Are you insane? I've earned this great bod," Rachel said. "All it takes is staying on the move. Being a poor starving traveler doesn't hurt either."

Liz agreed. "Yup, I can thank my parents for my great bone structure and naturally high metabolism." Ashley took in Liz's long svelte body. She was about five feet ten and as lean as they came. On the bright side, kids in school had probably called her "bean pole."

"Well, I am not going to leave my fate to a bunch of overprocessed airheads," Rachel said, standing up and stepping to the side of the pool. "I make my own rules and I will not be overlooked." She tossed her sunglasses onto her chair and dove into the pool with Luke and Tami.

Not to be outdone, others jumped into the pool too. Even book-smart Liz wasn't going to be left out.

"Come on, Ashley. Join the party," Liz urged as she jumped in.

Ashley sat on the sidelines and smiled at their antics. Everyone was having a great time. She couldn't help but laugh. Luke was having a ball as well. No longer cornered by any one person, he was part of a splashing-and-dunking party.

Ashley saw the opportunity to get away and be alone for a while, as the camera crews surrounded the pool. She really needed a break from the insanity, so she grabbed her towel and quickly snuck away for some solitary time.

The party went on for a couple of hours. Music continued to pump loudly from the sound system. Several tables laden with an amazing array of party food and partially finished beverages with tiny umbrellas sat forgotten. Under normal circumstances, this would have been a great party. But Luke felt claustrophobic surrounded by all the eager young beauties and he needed a break.

"Excuse me, darlin'. I'll be back in a minute." Luke peeled Jenny, the attractive cling-on, off his arm and excused himself to go inside to use the bathroom. Once inside and away from the noise and activity, he felt relieved. The girls' competitiveness astounded him. It was nice to be wanted, but this was ridiculous. It was worse than fan day at Lambeau Field. Well, almost. At least Security kept the people in line there. Here, he'd been thrown to the wolves.

Luke wandered through the house toward the back

doors and looked out over the pristine beach. He watched the waves roll into shore, and a sense of peace washed over him. He glanced back to the pool where all the contestants and the camera crews waited for his return. If he was lucky he might get five uninterrupted minutes before they noticed he was gone. There were just too many girls to keep straight. They were all beautiful and physically a ten. What more could a guy want? Except maybe a little breathing room instead of constantly being rubbed against, and given coy looks and a lot of fake laughter. This bachelor stint had sounded a lot easier than it was turning out to be.

He took one quick look to make sure the coast was clear and then snuck out the doors onto the back deck, and quickly took off down the beach. The sun glistened on the water and a gentle breeze brought the refreshing scent of sea air. He saw a lone beach umbrella farther down the beach. It was the perfect place to hide. He needed a few minutes of solitude to watch the ocean and gear up for the next few hours of social time.

As he walked up to the umbrella that looked empty from a distance, he noticed a lounge chair occupied by a pretty blond engrossed in a paperback novel. She looked quite content in her little paradise with a towel and a soda and the sun shining down on her. A light ocean breeze gently blew her hair around her face.

Not to be deterred from his goal to hide behind the umbrella, Luke approached and noticed that she looked familiar. "Hey, aren't you the girl who threw herself at my feet the other night?"

Startled, Ashley knocked the soda into her lap. She tried to look calm as cold liquid ran between her legs and soaked her bottom.

She'd been discovered.

"It was more of a launch," she replied, trying to look casual and not like the deserter she was. "By the way, you wore really nice shoes that night. I meant to mention it before." She smiled up at him.

Luke crossed his muscular arms over his chest. "Shouldn't you be over at the pool with the rest of the masses, trying to delve into all my inner secrets and position yourself for the next round?"

Ashley noted the hint of sarcasm in his voice, but was distracted by the incredible man before her. Luke stood to the side, forcing her to look up at him, but also blocking the bright sun from her eyes. He was over six feet of bare bronzed skin and toned in all the right places. His swim trunks hung low on his hips.

"Uh, oops, you caught me! I cannot tell a lie." She swallowed, distracted by the hunk of man before her. "I figured there was so much estrogen by the pool that no one would mind one less man-eating woman." She repositioned herself on the chair and tried to look re-laxed as she attempted to mop up the cold soda in which she sat. "Plus, I figured none of the girls would turn me in," she added with a bit of sarcasm. "They'd be happy to have more time with the man of the hour."

Luke raised his eyebrows at her cynical comment. Ashley couldn't seem to shut herself up. "So, look at this as a gift, allowing you more time to get acquainted with them. One less person you have to get to know." She hoped he would take the hint and move on.

"Really?" he said. His eyes seemed skeptical. "Seems to me you just wanted to get out here to work on your tan in private." His gaze moved leisurely over her body, from the tip of her nose down to her pale white legs. "Which, by the way, could use a lot of work. Do those legs ever see the light of day?"

Ashley was relieved she'd worn her beach wrap, and repositioned it around her waist to cover more skin. It was obvious that her legs hadn't seen sun in a very long time. She lived in the Midwest, with only a couple of months of summer. The rest of the year felt like a transition to and from winter.

"Hey, I like the pasty white look." She covered as much skin as possible. "You're lucky I'm not too sensitive or you might have really hurt my feelings."

"I am so sorry!" he replied in exaggerated contrition, not looking like he meant it. "Hey, do you mind if I sit down? I'd like to keep a low profile for at least a few minutes."

"Oh, so you're the one hiding!" she accused playfully. "That bad already?"

"No, it's not too bad," Luke answered, sounding weary. "It's just a little intense back there. I feel like the last beer at a frat party." He sat down on the end of the chair facing Ashley, a spark of interest in his eye. "Speaking of hiding, if I didn't know how bad your skin needed some sun, I'd say you were hiding as well. What's up? I thought you came here to win yourself a guy, to marry the bachelor."

"Yes, it appears that way, doesn't it? I mean the win-the-guy part." She tried to figure a way to quickly defuse the situation and get him off her trail. There was no telling when she'd be alone with him again. This might be her best opportunity to steer him away from her.

"I know I look pretty desperate," she said, smiling at herself. "Actually the truth is . . . No offense . . ." Ashley glanced at him out of the corner of her eye. "But you're not exactly my type."

"Is that so?" He laughed, obviously amused by her comment. "I'm crushed. In fact, I may have to return to the hungry pack of wolves back there just to build up my ego."

"Great." She fiddled with the fringe of her cover-up. "I was really enjoying the solitude away from all those cameras. And if you stay much longer they'll probably track you down. Then I'd be caught too, so please go build up your poor deflated ego," she teased. He was a lot of fun to talk to, particularly without the horde of women always on his trail.

"Okay, but before I go, I want to know what your type is. I mean, if it's not me then don't you think it's only fair to tell me what is?" Luke challenged with a smirk on his face. "After all those personality tests you took, we should be a potential perfect match. In fact, every girl here should be a potential perfect match."

"That's a funny thing, isn't it?" Ashley spoke softly, leaning forward. "I always cheat on tests. I guess this time it backfired on me. I got the wrong guy." She sat back again and spoke confidently. "So I thought I'd just turn this into a little vacation instead. Plus, it leaves you one less to choose from. So you see, I have just done you an incredible favor by giving you one less pursuer to hunt you down." She smiled brightly.

Luke leaned back on one arm and placed his leg next to Ashley's on the lounge chair. "Fine. You're using me for a vacation. But, tell me, what *is* your type?" He lowered his sunglasses down the bridge of his nose so that his intense blue eyes peered over the top, straight at her. "Satisfy me."

Ashley stared back and took a deep breath. She tried to remain unaffected after receiving his piercing gaze. "Well, let's see. I really like a serious professional," Ashley said.

"I'm a professional."

Ashley gave him a swift glare. "Not that kind of professional. Someone highly educated, not afraid to use his brain instead of his brawn."

"Did you know I have a degree in mechanical engineering from Duke?" he teased with a smirk.

She tried to ignore his long masculine leg resting against hers and continued, "He shouldn't be too muscular."

Luke looked down at his buff physique and raised his muscular arm to flex his bicep. He gave her another of his devilish grins. "I'm a wimp compared to a linebacker."

"I don't like a show-off," she returned, trying to act natural. "He must be intellectual, and proud of it. In fact, I'd like someone a little on the nerdy side. I find it really endearing."

With that Luke took off his sunglasses, then put them back on upside down, and in an odd nasal voice recited, "E equals M-C squared."

Laughing at how goofy he looked and sounded, Ashley whacked him on the arm with her paperback, which he grabbed from her. "Seriously, there is something very attractive about a nerdy guy who isn't walking around with all kinds of macho body confidence."

Luke gave her a cockeyed look. "Yeah, sure there is."

"Oh, and rich . . . He's got to be absolutely loaded," she added.

"Can't argue with that one." He grinned.

Trying to ignore him, she said, "I can't be tying myself down to some poor schmuck who isn't willing to drop the big bucks on me. You may have money, but it's small potatoes compared to what I want."

"I can see you have expensive tastes," he pointed out as he waved her dime-store novel in the air before tossing it back into her lap.

She attempted to ignore his accurate observation, and changed the subject. "I'm afraid it never would have worked out between the two of us."

He gave her a challenging look, as if to say, "So you think so, do you?"

"So sorry. I'm sure you'll find happiness somewhere along the way, but I'm just looking for someone a bit more . . . accomplished in life."

"I see," Luke replied. "Sounds as though I have a lot of work to do before I could begin to appeal to such a classy girl as you." He glanced down at the trashy novel lying on her soda-soaked lap. "So please, correct me if I'm wrong here, but basically you are taking up a spot the woman of my dreams might have filled. You are depriving some sweet young thing from having the opportunity of getting to know me."

"Yes, I suppose you're right, but think of it this way: I'm one less person to put pressure on you and look at you with innocent little puppy-dog eyes saying, 'Pick me, pick me,'" she mocked, doing her best whiny puppy imitation.

"Actually," Luke said in a soft, sexy voice as he leaned back onto one elbow, "I get more bedroom eyes from the women than I do puppy-dog looks. I guess they are appealing to my more masculine instincts."

"Ah, right," she replied, swallowing down her arousal at his low voice. "You do have quite a reputation as a ladies' man."

Ashley noticed the camera crew jogging down the beach toward them. "Oh great," she said. "They found me, I mean you! You have got to leave—now." She popped up from the soda-drenched chair and retied the wet beach wrap around her hips.

"I'm out of here." She turned to Luke once more. "Thanks for dropping by, Luke. I wish you the best in your quest to find that special someone."

Ashley grabbed her towel and book and quickly moved down the beach before the camera crews could catch up and corner her. Luke watched her hips sway as she escaped with her soggy beach wrap slapping against her milk-white thighs. He had come out to the beach for a breath of fresh air and been rewarded with much more. He'd met a stubborn woman declaring herself off the show.

Luke found Ashley refreshing. This show had become so intense, with each woman trying to tell him her life story and learn his in only a few hours. But here was Ashley, telling him to his face that he wasn't her type. He wasn't sure if it had ever happened before. This whole thing had just taken a new turn. Unknowingly, she'd started a whole new ball game. He had a surprise for her: Game on!

Luke wondered what her angle was. Everyone had one. Perhaps hers was to play coy and hard-to-get. Either way, she was a lot easier to talk to than most of the eligible women back by the pool. However, he found he was a bit annoyed at her not caring enough about him or the chance to get to know him.

Chapter Four

Another day, another date. Thank goodness she wasn't on it. Ashley woke up feeling sore all over. Liz took one look at her and started laughing. Rachel just shook her head with a look of pity. Ashley moved to the dresser mirror. Her face was beet red. She stretched her T-shirt to expose a painfully burned shoulder, the white strap mark proving her skin had once been something other than fire-engine red.

Just what she needed, another reason to feel inferior. Yesterday she'd been the only one with pasty white skin. Today she would stand out like a beacon.

Tami barreled down the hall shoving people out of her way.

"Who took my lip gloss?" Steam practically poured

out of her nose and ears. "So help me, Gwen, if I find 'Charged up Cherry' on your skinny little lips, I swear I'll scratch it off with my fingernails and there will be one less person to give a rose to!"

Ashley tried to move through the chaos. Gwen wiped her mouth on the inside hem of her dress. The women were getting ready for the next big rose ceremony. Tempers flared as the ladies rushed to prepare for the long night ahead of them. Ashley just wanted to escape the insanity and find a few minutes of peace and quiet.

Women rushed from room to room comparing notes about who was wearing what and how they should do their hair. Many rushed back to their rooms to do more. At the rate things were going, they would all end up with too much makeup and hairspray.

In the larger bathroom, beauty queen Shelby hogged the mirror. Huge hollow rollers covered her head. She looked like a giant air-head doll, but then she pretty much was. She stood in a skin-tight tank top, posing and posturing before the mirror, examining every angle as Kate tried to squeeze in long enough to apply her mascara without stabbing an eye.

"Do you think my left one is higher than my right?" Shelby asked, holding a breast in each hand. She lifted each one up and down. "Look, this one doesn't bounce as much as the other."

"So sue 'em," Kate said skeptically.

Ashley couldn't believe fourteen women could

scurry around so frantically for the big night, all of them aflutter at the prospect of five women being let go. It seemed like too many of them gone too soon. Most of them hadn't even had a group date with Luke.

"He can't possibly make a fair decision when we've only been on one date," said Jenny the snuggler.

"At least you've had a date," complained Melissa.

"Yeah, but I couldn't even get him alone. How can I possibly make the right impression when I can't get him alone?"

"What kind of impression did you have in mind?" asked Kris.

Looking sly and seductive, she answered, "Oh honey, the kind of impression that makes a man return for more."

Ashley's tolerance hit its limit. She edged through the group and snuck into her small bedroom and out onto the secluded balcony. Finally. A little peace and quiet. She took a deep calming breath to ease the stress. These women made her nuts. She gazed out over the trees at the setting sun. What a beautiful combination of pinks, ambers, and purples. A soft, warm breeze brought the scent of lilacs wafting through the air. After a few minutes, Ashley felt much more relaxed.

She could still hear the commotion inside, but it didn't bother her now. Even her own roommates, who normally acted down-to-earth, were getting ready with a high level of stress. Rachel had fallen for Luke on the very first date of the show. She did her best to act nonchalant, but with little success. Ashley hoped Rachel received a rose. Rachel was fun and adventurous and had been totally caught off guard by the game.

Ashley's view, however, hadn't changed. She still felt the whole thing was a joke, including most of the women; they represented some of the worst female stereotypes. Take Shelby. While very beautiful, she couldn't move past her beauty-pageant past. Everything was about how she looked and about winning the contest. She seemed confused about whether she was there to win her next crown or to meet a man with whom she could have a lasting relationship. Ashley hoped Luke saw through her.

Luke presented another interesting piece of the puzzle. He appeared to be a nice guy. Down-to-earth and well grounded. Yes, he looked great with an amazing body that could melt butter, but who could fault him that? Ashley shivered, thinking of him at the pool party, his tanned physique in low-slung swim trunks, his muscles rippling with each move he made.

He was nice to everyone, even though he didn't have much time. He had an engaging sense of humor and a great smile. Ashley had been the recipient of his smile a number of times now since their first introduction and their chance meeting on the beach.

Her real question concerning Luke was why he'd

agreed to do such a stupid show. He could have any woman he wanted, and yet he'd signed on for a reality show with all these women parading in front of him, trying to lure him with their feminine wiles. For a guy who spent so much time in front of the spotlight, why would he want more of it? Perhaps he was one of those people who needed to be the center of attention all the time. He didn't give off that impression, but who knew? She could be wrong.

She would ask Liz or Rachel to find out his real motivation to do the show. Ashley felt fairly confident that at least one of them would stay on a little longer. She, however, hoped her lack of a date with Luke and her blatant disinterest in him guaranteed her a ticket out of there and back to true reality. Back to the reality of putting her life together, starting with landing a real job, a job that involved no cameras and no harem of women. She couldn't wait. The thought of regaining her privacy would get her through tonight's rose ceremony.

Luke sat quietly on the balcony of his condo. The show put him up in style. The place was a bit pretentious for his tastes, with too much chrome and glass, but the large balcony was heaven. And what a view! The coastline and ocean stretched before him, as far as he could see. Huge, airy ferns filled the space, creating a casual, relaxed feel. It was well-furnished, with comfortable swivel rockers and small tables placed here and there so that he always had a spot to set his sports page.

The sun set slowly on the horizon. Luke's half-finished beverage hung easily in his hand as he contemplated the rose ceremony scheduled to start in about an hour. He'd expected the game to be much different. When his brother Mike had tricked him into going on the show, after he'd lost a bet, Luke had been ticked. He was sick and tired of his family and friends trying to get him to settle down. Heck, he was still young, and there was no reason he needed to give up bachelorhood. Granted, he lived a decadent life when it came to women, but hey, they were hard to avoid when you were a successful quarterback. A warm breeze moved through the fern fronds creating the illusion that they danced in their hanging pots. Over the water, pelicans soared across the water looking for the perfect moment to dive in and catch their prey—not unlike what the producers expected him to do with in the next several minutes.

Luke sighed. The show had been surprisingly fun so far. He couldn't complain about being handed two dozen women from which to pick and choose. The only problem was that he actually knew some of them now. He didn't quite know how to proceed. He wasn't used to seeing any one woman so often in this short a period of time.

His life usually consisted of practices, games, and travel during the season. In the off-season, he spent his time on the golf course with his buddies or at charity events for the dozens of causes he supported. The list of people wanting him to lend his name and face to their cause never ended. He met new people all the time. He didn't have to see them for very long, so brief interludes with ladies worked perfectly. No strings, no attachments. Love 'em and leave 'em—it wasn't just that it was almost the same as the name of this show, but it was his mantra.

What to do about tonight? Hmm. The obvious plan would be to keep the best-looking women in the game. He should keep himself surrounded with great eye candy. Then he supposed he should go for those with whom he had the most in common, someone athletic, who wouldn't be afraid to join him when he went golfing. Someone willing to get out and be active. Life was full of great adventures and he wanted to share them with a woman who had spirit.

That would make up the majority of the roses, but who to pick then? He disliked bossy or overly fussy women. It was one thing to be feminine and know how to use it, and another to act like a simpering, helpless fool. He looked out across the water and watched the sun as it sank beyond the ocean, creating the most spectacular wash of colors in the sky. Vivid purples and blues, pinks and reds layered and overlapped, creating an amazing masterpiece. He never saw anything like this in Wisconsin.

A smile came to his lips as Luke took another swig.

Of course! He would pick the challenging women. Nothing better to keep the game interesting. He tilted the bottle, guzzled the last bit and stood.

Time to play ball.

Ashley walked into the room that was filled with big lights and cameras. It was reminiscent of the first night, when everything was brand new and intimidating. While things still overwhelmed her, she now knew the drill. Instead of wearing a long formal gown, as she'd done on the first night, she chose a light floral dress. The hemline ended right at the bend of her knee, showing off a bit of leg, yet not too much. The dress gently tapered to her waist, with a diamond cutout revealing the tender skin of her back. She felt that she looked pretty nice—except for the brilliant color of her face. She did what she could with powder and concealer but tiny blisters covered her nose and her whole face felt tight and hot. Hopefully, Luke would take pity and not call her up to accept a rose. She could only imagine how red she'd look on camera.

The other contestants wore various levels of dress ranging from cocktail dresses to sundresses. As Ashley had expected, several women wore way too much makeup, particularly Jenny the snuggler and their roommate Gwen the crier. Gwen's eyeliner was so thick, if she started crying again, black rivers would run down her face and onto her light pink dress.

Rachel and Liz stood off to the side, checking out the competition.

"Look at them." Rachel pointed. "They're like vultures going in for the kill."

Luke stood on the other side of the room, not far from the entry. He leaned against the banister, hands in his pockets. The soft fabric of his tan trousers draped gently down his thighs and a black silky shirt hung to perfection from his broad shoulders. He bent his head down as he leaned forward to listen to something Cricket was saying. He wore a small smile on his lips as he listened politely and then replied. Luke didn't seem fazed a bit that he was surrounded by a group of women, each hoping to ensure they received a rose or could sway his decision if necessary. He acted relaxed and happy and looked amazingly hot, as usual. Ashley could watch him all night. Luke flashed a devastating smile at her. Ashley realized he'd caught her staring and quickly turned away. At least no one could see her blush through her sunburn.

After another twenty minutes, the producers placed each of the women in a semicircle so that the cameras could easily cover everyone. Ashley ended up in the back row. Rachel was right in front of her and Liz stood in the back row, within eye contact of Ashley. Luke stood next to Clay the dorky host and a small table of roses. There still appeared to be a lot of roses on that table.

Ashley wore a pair of light gray sandals with braided leather straps. They were much more comfortable than the designer stilettos she'd had strapped to her feet on opening night. She hoped that tonight would go much quicker, and that her feet wouldn't suffer so much.

"Good evening, ladies. You look absolutely delicious." Clay rubbed his hands together. "We are so excited about this round of cuts, aren't we, Luke?" he said, nodding eagerly to Luke as though they were best buddies. Luke rewarded him with a blank stare. Clay always stretched things out and made them all suffer as long as possible. After sucking up, he turned it over to Luke to hand out the coveted roses.

The air in the room tensed as Luke stepped forward. As the others stood anxiously waiting to learn their fate, Ashley scooted to the side so that she was mostly hidden by Rachel, who teetered in her high heels.

Luke held the first rose in his hand and looked directly at the group. "Tami," he said with no hesitation.

It figures. No doubt why he picked her first.

Tami purred her way up to accept the rose and gave him a satisfied smile, looking as though she'd just caught a mouse.

"Will you accept this rose?" He looked at her with smoldering eyes.

"Oh yeah, baby." She returned the look.

He leaned forward to kiss her on the cheek. She turned her face in time to catch the kiss on her lips. Slow and moist.

A collective release was heard in the room as the mood of the women deflated. Tami stepped to the side and caressed her neck with the newly won rose. Filming paused while the lip gloss was wiped from Luke's mouth.

Next he offered a rose to Cricket, a pretty but quiet girl, then Jenny the snuggler. When he said Rachel's name, she just about jumped out of her heels. Ashley hoped it worked out well for her. She was such a sweetheart.

With a huge grin on her face, Rachel walked up to receive her rose. Luke rewarded her with one of his trademark smiles. After handing her the rose, he kissed her on the cheek, and Rachel looked like she'd died and gone to heaven as she joined the other rose recipients.

Unfortunately, with Rachel out of the lineup, Ashley stood in full view of Luke. Out of sight meant out of mind, and Ashley definitely wanted to stay out of Luke's mind.

Next, he called forward Megan, Kate, and Shelby, the Texas pageant girl. Shelby didn't seem the right fit for Luke, but apparently he liked big hair and heavy makeup application. Or maybe her Southern drawl did the trick. Some guys were suckers for Southern girls, and Luke grew up in the South. No, it probably wasn't the hair.

Seven girls held roses, which left eight girls yet to have their fates determined. Three more would be picked and five would be left with nothing but a plane ticket home. Luke took his time looking over the group. Most of them did their best to look irresistible and yet nonchalant. Except Ashley and Gwen. Gwen's lower lip quivered, her eyes were glassy with unshed tears, and she continued to wring her hands on her dress. Ashley, on the other hand, hoped to blend in with the background.

"Liz," Luke announced.

Ashley turned her head and gave Liz a congratulatory smile. Both Rachel and Liz had made it to the next round. Perhaps Luke could recognize quality women.

He took another pause looking over the last of the girls. Two roses remained. He looked up at Lindsey, the money-hungry gold digger. Then to Gwen, the crier. Ashley figured he'd run out of good candidates and was trying to pick the lesser of two evils.

"Gwen," he said.

"Oh my God!" squealed Gwen as she ran to him. "Thank you, thank you, thank you." She plucked the rose from his hand and jumped up and down in her excitement. She rushed over to the group of rose-bearing women, then suddenly turned and ran back to Luke. She jumped up to peck a kiss on his cheek and then, nearly breathless with elation, ran back to the group, gasping as though she'd just completed a marathon instead of a ten-foot sprint.

Luke smiled at her excitement. He was having a good time.

Slowing the pace, he surveyed the group of six remaining. He studied each face.

Ashley wanted desperately to look away, as she'd done in school when she hadn't wanted to get called on. Instead, she stood still, eyes focused down, and tried to appear pleasant but uninterested. Inside, her stomach churned. Her mind raced, thinking, *Pass me by, pass me by*. Behind her back, she anxiously picked at her fingernails, wishing the whole ordeal was over. The bright lights of the cameras beat down on her.

Clay stepped forward. He looked somberly at the remaining women and then at Luke. "This is the final rose."

Moron.

Luke picked up the final rose. He focused on Lindsey, then shifted his gaze to Ashley. He looked away, as though deep in thought, then smiled and said, "Ashley."

Teeth clenched, Ashley pasted a pleasant expression on her face and stepped forward to accept the rose.

As she attempted to take the rose, Luke held it fast and raised an eyebrow at her in challenge. She could almost hear him say, "Not your type? We'll see about that." He leaned forward to give her a kiss on the cheek and instead whispered in her ear, "Nice burn."

He released the rose. She stepped away to join the "winners." Clay immediately stepped forward to thank the other girls for participating and offered them a brief chance to say good-bye to Luke.

Ashley was stunned and disappointed. She had looked forward to getting back to reality. The longer she stayed on the show, the more employment opportunities she lost out on.

Rachel rushed over to congratulate her.

"Can you believe it? He picked you."

"Yeah, isn't that great?" Ashley gave her a weak smile, wondering why she was so surprised. "But I feel kind of like a reject getting picked after the crier."

"No way," Rachel said brightly. "He saved the best for last!"

Liz joined them and watched the losers say their clingy good-byes. "You have nothing to feel bad about. Look at who didn't get picked. Lindsey was only after his money and he knew it. The others were either too annoying or too desperate." She gestured toward the departing group. "He was weeding out the riffraff. You have just as much a chance as anyone else here."

"Great," Ashley said. Not what she wanted to hear. No matter how she looked at it, she was stuck here for a while longer.

Chapter Five

T he taping always lasted late into the night, and after all the hoopla and good-byes were finally over, the remaining women sat up with Luke celebrating the next leg of the contest. They sat around the great room to get better acquainted. Jenny the snuggler sat on the floor next to Luke, poised for any attention he might throw her way. Everyone else sat on furniture to digest the evening's events and revel in the knowledge that they were still in the game.

Ashley definitely wanted out and back to the true reality of her life, but she did feel a little bit special to have been selected. After all the recent rejections from her cheating boyfriend and her job at the insurance company, it was nice to be wanted. As long as Luke didn't want her for much longer. She did have a life to rebuild, one that didn't involve cameras, lighting, or a hunky football player.

The next day turned out to be low-key. Luke took Jenny and Gwen to the famous San Diego Museum of Art. Ashley didn't see Luke as much of an arts man, but perhaps he was more than what he seemed.

Liz, Rachel, and Ashley were hanging out on the back deck overlooking the sandy beach and distant waves when Kate, a gorgeous law student, popped her head out a window to announce the arrival of more date mail. They followed her in to get the skinny. Kate hopped up on the kitchen counter facing the rest of the group, her lean athletic legs swinging to and fro. She matter-of-factly ripped open the envelope and began to read:

> *Strap on your skis and grab your poles.*
> *Five of you are joining me in Vail.*
> *Your ride leaves early, so don't be late.*
> *This adventure is for Megan, Cricket, Liz,*
>   *Ashley, and Kate.*

A quick smile came over Kate's face. "All right! We're going skiing."

Torn between convincing herself that she didn't want to go and feeling excited that she was actually going on a date, Ashley glanced at Liz, who was also getting her first date, and Ashley saw her look of panic.

"What's wrong?" Ashley whispered.

Looking around desperately, Liz replied. "I can't go. I'm terrified of skiing."

The excitement and anticipation of leaving the heat of southern California and experiencing the cool temps and white powder of Vail made the morning pass quickly. Ashley could see Liz's nervousness. Her new friend had been involved in a minor skiing accident during high school, and now she avoided the sport. Though Liz really wanted to be on the date, she kept trying to find ways out of the skiing. Twice she approached the producers about staying in the lodge, but no go. Most likely, they intended to add more drama by showcasing her fear.

"Don't worry. I have a plan guaranteed to help you relax today." Ashley smiled as she patted her carry-on bag.

"What's that? Crashing the plane?" Liz hugged herself.

"Trust me."

The limo pulled onto the tarmac where a private plane was parked with the door open. A pilot and flight attendant awaited their arrival.

"Wow, this feels like the movies when the tycoon takes his new girlfriend to lunch in some exotic place." Megan boarded the plane eagerly. Ashley followed.

Everything was leather or gold. Huge leather seats. Beautiful wall sconces every four feet. Leather couches and loveseats were set close to the front of the plane with small oak tables next to them for beverages and snacks. The smell of freshly brewed coffee welcomed the group, along with the sweet aroma of baked cinnamon rolls and croissants.

Ashley directed Liz to a pair of seats two rows behind Luke and Kate. This way he couldn't easily see her when he looked or spoke to the other women, and Ashley could sit near the window tucked out of sight from him. Her plan was to have a good time while allowing the other vultures plenty of room to circle their prey.

The turbulent flight kept everyone from moving to the luxurious leather couches. Despite the upheaval, the flight attendant served freshly squeezed orange juice in crystal and delicious breakfast fare on china. Ashley wondered how much the flight cost the network. Then again, the plane probably belonged to the network, so maybe it wasn't much of an investment after all.

After the short flight, a shuttle bus delivered them promptly to Vail Village. Snow dusted the rooftops and window sills, but the sidewalks and streets were clear. There was a festive feel to the air as people milled around, window shopping in the exclusive stores or enjoying a late breakfast in one of the enticing little chalets.

The producer directed them into a trendy ski shop on Bridge Street, where a staff waited to outfit each of them with the latest in ski-bunny fashions. There were sporty one-piece ski outfits, stylish jackets, fur pieces and more than Ashley could imagine people would want to wear skiing.

After being shooed into a dressing room with a pile of clothing, she stepped out with a grimace.

"I can't wear this," Ashley said.

"You look fabulous," replied the sales clerk.

"You don't understand. Where I come from, skiing means you put on as many layers of clothing as possible. I wear padded ski pants and a long down-filled jacket that covers my rear end."

"No, no, no. If you're going to ski Vail, you must dress Vail," the clerk said in her singsong voice.

"On top of that is a gator, sort of like a triple-wide headband. You pull it down over your head to keep your neck warm and it doubles as a face mask."

The woman continued to peruse Ashley, brushing imaginary lint off her lycra-covered bottom.

"Of course"—Ashley went on talking, mostly to herself—"an actual headband keeps your hair back and warms your forehead. If done correctly, no one recognizes you. Looking cute plays absolutely no role in Wisconsin skiing."

Here, under the tutelage of the ski shop style masters, she realized she wasn't in Wisconsin anymore. Ashley found herself dressed in skintight black Lycra ski bibs cut out tightly below her small bosom, which pleasantly made it appear much larger but unfortunately drew the eye there as well. The rich persimmon-colored turtleneck hugged her body as well, and set off the highlights in her hair. Then she donned a form-fitting jacket that ended just below her waist and was accented with a small bit of black fur around the neck. The jacket zipped only a third of the way up, which further showed off her curves. She felt naked! "Really, don't you think I'd look much better in something from Lands' End? How 'bout Eddie Bauer? I don't do designer very well."

The woman stood back, admiring her creation.

Pleading further, Ashley asked, "How about one of those big, bulky, long wool sweaters? I get really cold and I need a lot more insulation."

The savvy saleswoman wouldn't budge. "It's a beautiful day. In this outfit, you won't be cold—you'll be melting the snow."

They had designer duds to push and Ashley was just another body to exploit. *Someone, please save me.*

As Ashley stood in front of the three-way mirror, mournful over her sex-kitten look, Liz popped into view glowing over her sassy white ski outfit. She wore the cutest hat, with white fur around the edge and matching fur on her collar and cuffs. *Poor dead bunny.* Her long dark hair hung like silk down her back, framing her lovely face and accentuating her big brown eyes and pouty red mouth.

"This is so not fair!" Ashley turned to get a full

view of her. "You look like an A-list movie star. I look like a D list nobody, as in 'Vicky Takes Vail!' "

"Isn't it gorgeous?" Liz beamed, catching her reflection in the mirror. "I've never felt more stunning. It even makes me less worried about the ski hill."

"Look at me!" complained Ashley. "It shows everything!" She kicked herself for not losing those extra few pounds.

"Oh relax. You look sexy, babe," Liz cajoled.

"I don't want to look sexy. I want to crawl under a rock, or better yet a horse blanket. Look, your ski jacket even covers your bum." Liz's coat went down slightly past her hips and flared out, so there was only a hint of her bottom showing beneath. Liz turned from side to side, peering over her shoulders to admire herself.

Each of the other women seemed quite comfortable in their various levels of overpriced designer ski duds. Ashley felt they carried it off with much more panache and style than she. She, on the other hand, couldn't walk comfortably with her pants riding up. It made her feel oddly aware of herself and a little bit naughty.

Standing in the back of the group to hide her overexposed body, she saw Luke saunter around the clothes racks from the men's side of the shop.

Wow! Maybe tight ski pants aren't such a bad thing.

He wore formfitting bibs with a charcoal black turtleneck. His jacket flashed electric blue with accents of black throughout, emphasizing his tan sculpted face. So maybe hanging out around Luke all day, looking like he did, might not be bad at all. Nope, not at all.

Everyone prepared to hit the slopes. When no one was looking, Ashley grabbed her flask from her bag and put the leather strap over her head, then tucked it into the crook of her jacket.

Ashley watched puffy clouds drift in stunning blue skies over the inviting snow-covered slopes. The temperatures were a mild thirty degrees. Cricket, Ashley, and Kate had skied enough growing up to be totally comfortable. Luke confessed he preferred a golf course to a ski hill any day.

At the chairlift Luke and Kate went first, Cricket and Megan followed, and Liz and Ashley brought up the rear. The camera crews waited, one at the base of the hill and one at the top. Ashley hoped they knew how to ski.

As they waited for their turn at the lift, Liz's nerves escalated.

"I can't do this."

"Sure you can. I'll help you," Ashley reassured her. "Just take a deep breath and relax. It's like riding a bike."

"It took me a whole summer to learn to ride a bike."

"See them?" Ashley pointed to the couple next in line. "As soon as the chair passes, they just glide into place with one push of the poles. Nice and smooth. You can do this." Ashley talked to her slowly and reassuringly, as if Liz was a child who needed coaxing to try something new.

"Are you ready?"

Liz nodded nervously. "Okay, I'm ready. Now I just glide."

"That's right."

They settled onto the chairlift with a huge sigh of relief from Liz.

"Okay, now the reward." Ashley pulled the flask from her jacket. She had tucked it under her arm and next to her breast, the only spot with any extra room. "Here, drink this."

Looking at her, Liz asked, "What is it?"

"Trust me. It's guaranteed to calm nerves on any ski hill."

Liz eyed her skeptically and hesitated.

"Come on and drink up, Evel Knievel. You need to relax so you don't embarrass yourself." Ashley unscrewed the top. "Liquid courage, and it can't be beat! Listen, if it makes it any easier, I'll join you. I could use some, what with my having to wear this getup."

"All right, if you really think it will help." Liz took the flask from Ashley and tipped it up, pouring the liquid into her mouth. She swallowed and started coughing and choking. "Is this hot chocolate?" she croaked.

Ashley giggled. "It's a combination of dark chocolate, hot cocoa powder, and steamed milk."

Liz took another drink and savored the flavor. "This is really good."

Ashley stole the flask back and took a drink. "Guaranteed to cure anything." She smacked her lips, then tucked the flask under her coat and prepared to dismount the chairlift.

Fortunately, the first run was a green beginners' hill. Several of the group hadn't been on skis for a while and were happy to start slowly. They surrounded Luke, looking around awkwardly until he said, "What the heck, it's only snow" and led the way.

Everyone followed. Ashley stayed with Liz while her friend found her ski legs. They glided down a nice gradual slope. Nothing scary. The day was gorgeous with almost no wind. Ashley slalomed gracefully down the hill, the sun on her face and the wind blowing through her hair. The saleswoman was right. She felt like a vision in her sexy black outfit.

Everyone was in great spirits as they lined up for the chairlift again. This time Luke sat with Cricket, and Ashley stayed with Liz. As soon as they settled on the lift, the flask reappeared. They passed it back and forth twice before they got off. Liz became more confident and steady on her skis with each run, or perhaps the sugar high was having the desired effect, and she just wasn't as worried.

After the next successful hill, they found a different chairlift that took them farther up the mountain and dropped them off at a beautiful chalet overlooking the ski hills and neighboring mountain peaks. The majestic snow-covered mountains in the distance jutted up into the blue sky, demanding attention. Having grown up in the Midwest, where there were no mountains, no oceans, and no deserts, Ashley couldn't help but be awed by the landscape. Wisconsin was beautiful, but nothing like the majesty and power that nature had created here.

They removed their skis and entered the Swiss-themed chalet. Inside, a fire blazed in the center of the room. A huge bar lined one entire wall, surrounded with tables. The décor included broken ski tips hung throughout the building.

Ashley nudged Liz. "Should we add ours to the collection before we leave?"

"Sure, why not?" Liz smiled.

The group followed one of the producers up to a private loft area where the camera crew set up. All of the hats, ski gloves, and jackets came off. Ashley no longer felt concerned about her ski-bunny outfit and comfortably slid the jacket off as she approached the table. She couldn't help but notice Luke gazing at her as he held a chair for Megan. Ashley usually kept a low profile, but this outfit was anything but. The fresh air had exhilarated her and the warm tingling in her face told her that her cheeks must be very rosy indeed. Ashley slipped out of her boots as well.

The waitress arrived to collect their orders for beverages.

Lunch turned out to be the highlight of the day, with a fun combination of people. Some of the women vied heavily for Luke's attention, but Ashley and Liz weren't concerned. Ashley didn't want his attention. The joking and teasing about each person's skiing ability went on as they enjoyed a relaxing and entertaining lunch.

They returned to the slopes in great spirits, Ashley and Liz in especially fine form. It was Liz's turn to sit with Luke on the chairlift, since he picked a different woman each time. Ashley gave her the thumbs-up as she joined Luke. Liz looked stunning, and Ashley was sure Luke would be entranced by her striking beauty and great personality.

The ski runs became longer, and the one they skied now was a blue intermediate run. When the group approached the end of the run, Ashley held back. She felt a bit of false bravado and decided to spray the group at the bottom of the hill with snow. She came straight down the hill without slowing; the faster the speed, the better the effect would be. As she neared the waiting group at full speed, panic lit their faces. She leaned hard into a tight turn at the last second and skidded expertly toward them. The spray created a huge arc of snow crystals shooting in all directions. She covered them literally from head to toe. Usually when she pulled this trick, she managed to stop directly in front of the skier. Not this time. She slid right into Liz.

Okay, maybe it was more of a slam.

Ashley tried not to hit too hard, but didn't want to spear Liz with a ski pole in the process. Her momentum caused Liz to fall into Cricket, and then Cricket into Kate, and so on, until she wiped out the entire group, including Luke. In moments, the whole group lay in a giant snow-covered heap at the base of the hill. Passing skiers didn't bother to stop. Instead of being horrified, Ashley began to laugh. Liz joined her, laughing as though it was the funniest thing that had ever happened.

Getting up, Kate tangled her skis with Megan's. Ashley, the only one not trapped under another skier, couldn't move because she was laughing so hard and trying not to wet her fancy ski pants. Luke lay buried under a couple of bodies, numerous skis, poles, and spandex-covered legs.

It took a couple of attempts, but finally they stopped giggling long enough to get untangled. Of course, the camera crew recorded the entire escapade and laughed right along with them. Once they were back on their feet, skis reattached, Luke motioned for the others to move ahead to the chairlift, then slid up to Ashley.

"Your turn," he said, piercing her with a knowing stare. He gestured her to join him on the chairlift.

Ashley felt like a kid caught with her hand in the cookie jar. She gave him an innocent smile as she slid smoothly past him into the lift line, acting like nothing was amiss.

"So, what's up?" He gazed down at her from only a few inches away, his firm mouth curled.

"Sorry, I guess I lost control back there," she replied, looking straight ahead.

"No, I mean what's going on?" He looked at her conspiratorially.

Ashley feigned innocence.

Luke gave her a sideways glance. "Your turn." He held his arm out to direct her toward the chairlift.

Ashley glided forward smoothly to the lift. She could feel Luke's eyes admiring her sexy ski outfit.

He joined her, and together they turned toward the approaching chair and sat. As Ashley settled herself, Luke examined her closely, then reached into her tight little jacket and pulled the leather strap to the flask.

"Okay, now I understand." He gave her an accusatory stare.

"It's not for me."

"Is that so?"

"Really, it's for Liz. She was afraid to ski and I knew a little boost would loosen her up."

"Well she's not the only one loosened up." He'd just discovered a new angle to her personality.

She nodded. "Yup, did you notice how relaxed she is now compared to her first run?" Luke watched her try to talk her way out of the situation. "She's a natural. Not a care in the world." Ashley swung her arms open wide.

He quickly put out his arm, as if to keep her from leaning forward and off the chairlift. "Whoa there! Let's keep you on the chairlift, okay?"

"Sorry. I guess we got a little carried away. I didn't mean to cause a scene with my snow spraying—it just sort of happened."

Luke stretched an arm around her shoulders and leaned his head close, enjoying the view her sexy outfit offered. "I'm disappointed you didn't share some of it with me." He noticed how relaxed she became when the cameras weren't around.

A big smile spread across her face as she looked up into his eyes. "By all means! What's mine is yours. You are the guest of honor here. Please help yourself." She opened the top of the flask and nodded for him to drink. He lifted it into the air and the liquid streamed smoothly into his opened mouth.

Luke began to choke. "It's hot chocolate, but not even hot."

Ashley grinned. "Gee, what did you think it was?"

Luke eyed her and gestured with the flask. "I never drink alone."

She took the challenge and, leaning back into the welcome crook of his arm, opened her mouth. He gently touched her lower lip with the edge of the flask opening and raised it high as he poured the rich liquid between her parted lips.

Luke sat mesmerized at her surrender. She deeply inhaled the taste of the drink and the pure mountain air. Her cheeks were rosy in the coolness of the day.

Luke replaced the cap and returned the flask to the protection of her bosom. He leaned forward and placed his moist lips against hers, tenderly sealing their drink with a kiss. He sensed her momentary surprise, and felt her relax in his arms as she welcomed his advances. He tasted the sweet chocolate on her lips. A small moan came from the back of her throat. Luke pulled away and watched her eyes flutter open, wide and innocent. He felt her warm breath upon his cheek.

Luke was entranced by this unusual beauty. She acted uninterested and tried to avoid him. She even said he wasn't her type and she wanted to get off the show. But whenever he got her alone and cornered her, he saw her sexy, fun side.

His lips parted slowly from hers. "Not your type, huh?"

They had reached the pinnacle of the mountain. Ashley turned to him, visibly disturbed. She shook her head. "It's all downhill from here."

Chapter Six

"I wish it were me tonight," Gwen said longingly as she dipped her speared meat into the hot oil to cook.

The women feasted on fondue around a low table in the great room. Liz and Kate were out with Luke on another date. The rest had settled in for an evening of relaxation.

"Me too," drawled Shelby, nibbling on a crisp piece of zucchini. "I can't get enough of that man!"

Not me, thought Ashley, glad she'd been left alone for a while and away from his piercing stares that always seemed to see too much. After the antics on the ski trip, Ashley was happy to hide back in the security of the mansion. She couldn't get Luke—or the way his lips had felt when he'd kissed her—out of her mind.

Each time the image popped into her mind her belly tingled and her toes curled up in a happy sort of way.

"I wish he'd kiss me," said Jenny with a far-off look as she prepared her skewer of steamed broccoli for the cheese fondue.

"He didn't kiss you?" asked Shelby, amazed but with a hint of satisfaction in her voice.

Most of them seemed surprised at Jenny's comment. It appeared as if they'd all received a kiss from Luke. Suddenly Ashley's intoxicating kiss on the chairlift didn't seem so hot. Apparently the man would lock lips with anything that moved. Except Jenny.

"Well, no, but it doesn't mean anything," defended Jenny. "He doesn't go around kissing everyone." She hesitated. "Does he?" She turned to Cricket for an answer.

Cricket gave her a nervous smile and shrugged her shoulders, a guilty look on her face.

Jenny swallowed and looked down at her broccoli, blinking back tears.

"Oh honey, it's all right," added Shelby, patting Jenny's hand. "The timing must have been off."

"That's right," crooned Tami in her haughty, overconfident way. "It's all about the timing. Of course, whenever I'm with Luke, it's time."

Tami crossed her legs as she leaned back into the plush cushions on the couch and flicked her tongue across her collagen-filled upper lip. "Let me tell you, that man has the moves and he knows how to use them."

"Are you sure those were his moves and not yours?" asked Shelby, with the perfect hint of Southern sarcasm.

Ashley caught Rachel's eye and winked in agreement. Tami glared her darkly shadowed eyes at Shelby.

If looks could kill . . .

"Gee, Tami," interrupted Rachel politely as she picked at the hot meat on her skewer. "Slapping and scratching are the only moves I saw you make on our fishing date, and that was at the bugs swarming all over you." Rachel nibbled at the meat. "I could be wrong, but Luke didn't seem too impressed."

On an earlier date, Rachel and Tami had joined Luke on a fishing trip. They'd left the mansion at 4:30 A.M. to drive to the boondocks and sit in a boat for six hours.

Tami had worn a cute little halter top and miniskirt along with her designer perfume. It'd turned out to be more than just a nice scent. According to Rachel, the perfume had attracted biting flies, gnats, and mosquitoes. Luke offered her bug spray a number of times, but Tami had said there was no way she would ever spray something that smelled so vile on her body. By the end of the trip Tami had gotten covered in bite welts up and down her shapely legs and even on her previously well-made-up face.

After the date Rachel and Luke had struggled to keep straight faces as they'd filed in behind Tami, who'd stomped her way upstairs as her dainty little handbag swung to the beat of her rage.

The rest of the group had stood in stunned silence to see the beautiful Tami with her feathers ruffled. There had been a general air of happiness to see her put out for a change.

Tami aimed daggers at Rachel for reminding her of this low point.

The dunking and nibbling continued. The women moved from the hot oil and the cheese fondue to the melted chocolate complete with strawberries, bananas and angel food cake. They became more relaxed as the night wore on.

"So, what do you think Luke wants in a woman?" Cricket wondered aloud as she cozied into a pile of pillows with a plate of chocolate-laden fruit.

"Great looks," blurted Shelby, biting into a plump, juicy strawberry.

"Brains," added Rachel thoughtfully.

"Affection," Jenny said hopefully.

"Personality?" squeaked Gwen.

The room went silent. They looked at Gwen in pseudohorror, and then all burst into laughter at once, including Gwen.

"He wants a woman he can get close to." Tami ran her hands sensually over her neck and shoulders, moving down over her flat stomach and hips.

Ashley could imagine that. It certainly supported his playboy image. He was so not her type—she needed to remember that.

"Ashley, what do you think?" Tami asked, interrupting her private Luke thoughts. Ashley knew the witch wanted her to admit her attraction to him.

"Oh no. I am *not* going there." The last thing she needed was to talk about Luke in front of the others, not to mention the pesky cameras set off in the corners as though they weren't really there catching every word. "You can leave me out of this discussion."

"He wants a woman he can tell what to do, like a player on a football team," giggled another.

"Yes, exactly!" agreed Jenny.

"Actually, he wants a woman who's a challenge," announced Meg with a voice of authority. "Someone he can meet eye-to-eye."

Meg was an interesting and beautiful creature. She was into all kinds of kooky psychic stuff. She always talked about energy and spirits, which got her a lot of questionable looks from the other girls. Her beautiful curly auburn hair surrounded her face in a whimsical cinnamon swirl.

"It's not my eyes I want him meeting," Shelby said, gazing down with satisfaction at her ample cleavage.

Ignoring the comment, Meg continued. "He wants a self-assured woman who won't back down all the time. He doesn't want someone he can walk all over. He wants an equal partner in life."

Each woman pondered Meg's analysis. Perhaps she was right.

"But he also wants a woman who is not afraid to take over. A confident woman," Meg continued matter-of-factly.

"Holy moly," Rachel murmured.

The group stared at Meg in wonderment.

"Where'd you come up with that?" Ashley encouraged her to continue.

"I did a reading."

"A what?"

"I did a card reading on him the other night. Kind of like Tarot cards, but for love. It makes sense."

Right. Of course. Now it makes sense. Confused looks filled the room.

"He's a powerful and confident man who enjoys control."

No argument there. He exuded control and confidence.

"However, he is also a sensitive soul who wants and needs to be loved and cared for." Meg seemed unaware of the odd looks directed her way. "He is wild, but he's also responsible. He wants it all." She shrugged her shoulders.

"Who doesn't?" Tami pointed out.

"No kidding. I could go for that," agreed Jenny.

"Wow, you're good. You came up with all that from a deck of cards?" Cricket asked in amazement.

"Mm-hmm. It's all in the interpretation, but it was pretty straightforward."

"I need a deck of those cards," said Gwen as she sat back against the couch cushions.

Chapter Seven

Tami and Shelby were out by the pool, working on their tans and future melanomas, while Ashley sat with Liz and a few others in the kitchen, drinking coffee and eating breakfast. Most of the girls ate fresh fruit or cereal. Ashley found a half-empty bag of Cheetos and devoured them with delight.

The casual chitchat and munching were suddenly interrupted by the sound of a commotion in the other room. In walked three cameramen armed and loaded. Clay, the anti-host, wore a sneaky grin as he appeared in the doorway with bachelor extraordinaire Luke, who looked fresh, crisp, and wide awake. It was obvious that the two men were prepared for this impromptu gathering, even if no one else was.

Ashley sat frozen, a Cheeto halfway to her mouth.

Everyone at the table stopped what they were doing and exchanged curious glances. Luke never showed up unannounced or without a big prearranged to-do. Something was up.

"Morning, ladies!" Luke said as he took in their various stages of undress and relaxed morning ritual. "I thought I'd come by to see what happens in the mornings when I'm not here." He pulled up a chair, as if ready to join their coffee klatch and gossip.

The back door opened as the others were rounded up. Meg spent her mornings on the beach doing yoga and clearing her aura. Tami and Shelby spent each day out by the pool. They all entered with the same curious, confused expressions on their face.

Luke's eyes roamed over the glistening bodies of Tami and Shelby. "You're looking well today."

Tami flashed Luke a sizzling look.

"What's going on?" Meg asked, moving into the room.

Cameras rolling, Clay stepped forward, his chest puffed up. "Actually, Luke, we're not here just to see how the ladies spend their mornings. We have a great surprise for all of you."

Several of the women squealed and jumped up and down in anticipation. Luke, eyes veiled with suspicion, stared at Clay.

"In a few minutes there will be an impromptu rose ceremony and four of you will be going home."

Silence filled the room. Shocked faces turned to each other for answers. It was obvious that the news was a surprise to Luke as well. He was quiet and pensive.

"So, without further ado, I'd like everyone to step into the great room. We're ready to begin," said Clay.

There was an instant barrage of objections and questions.

"We need more time to prepare."

"I haven't had a single date yet!"

"Why now? Can't we go change and get ready?"

"How many roses will there be?"

"I am not going out there until I brush my teeth."

Clay appeared to be flying high with all the turmoil around him. "Ladies, I know this is a big surprise, but it will be fun. You all look beautiful in your natural state. Plus, it gives Luke an opportunity to see what you look like when you're not dressed up with your hair and makeup done."

Ashley peered down at her old gray sweatpants cut off to sleeping shorts and her stretched-out, faded yellow tank top. Her hair was mussed from sleep, telltale residue from yesterday's mascara lay under her eyes, and she wasn't wearing a bra.

"I'm ready. Let's go," boasted Tami, parading herself in front of Luke. She wore a hot pink bikini, her body oiled up like a greased pig, a stylish clip holding up her hair.

* * *

Luke pushed Clay off into the corner. He was not happy. Clay looked like he'd pee his pants any second as Luke towered over him.

"What the heck is going on?" Luke demanded. "And why wasn't I told about this?" All six feet two, two hundred pounds of powerful anger was focused on Clay.

"The producers planned it," Clay answered, his smile weak. His eyes darted around. "It'll be great for ratings."

"This is my life, you arrogant little jerk. Don't pull this crap on me." Luke tried unsuccessfully to keep his voice down. "The least that I—and they—deserve is an honest chance. How can I send more home? I'm not ready to do this. I haven't even thought it through yet."

"Well, I guess you'll just have to work more quickly in the future. Just pick the six prettiest ones. That's what I'd do," Clay said.

Luke wanted to smack the smug expression off the weasel's face.

"Don't play with my life. I will not be made a fool of." Luke poked him in the chest with each word. "Don't screw with me! Got it?" Luke glared at the little man.

Clay scanned the room, looking for help. "Hey, don't kill the messenger. It wasn't my decision."

Jim, the producer, noticed their confrontation and walked over to intercede. "Relax, Luke. Just go with the flow. No one is out to get you. Remember, we're all here to have fun and make a great show. You can't make a bad choice out there. They're all winners."

Luke took a deep breath in an effort to calm himself and regain control of the situation. He'd been thrown into bad circumstances in the past and had always pulled through. The producer was right—the women were all nice enough. He was a quarterback and used to having control.

Today he'd just have to punt.

The women were quickly ushered into the great room while crews put the final touches on lighting and sound. The producer moved to stage the girls in two rows. They were all in different levels of panic and frustration as they tried to fix their appearances with nothing to aid them.

Rachel pulled Ashley aside. "Promise to stay in touch when this is over, okay?"

"Sure, of course I will." Ashley wondered what was on her mind. "Why do you say that?"

"Well, I know you and Luke haven't really hit it off and you don't seem very interested in being here anyway. Don't get me wrong—I think you're great. I just wanted to be sure I had a chance to say good-bye."

"All right," she answered as she walked away awkwardly, not sure what to think. Apparently Rachel assumed she'd be off today. Maybe so.

Ashley ran her fingers through her sleep-mussed hair, knowing how awful she would look next to Tami and Shelby. The rest of the girls were in various modes of casual wear. Meg wore a loose cover-up, and Kate had just returned from her morning run and wore a co-ordinated Nike running ensemble. Liz and Rachel were in their pj's, but had at least brushed their hair before they'd come down.

Ashley stood in the front row feeling totally humiliated. One by one she sucked each finger to get rid of the built-up cheese coating from her Cheeto breakfast. She glanced up and noticed Luke next to the rose table watching her every move. Amusement glinted in his eyes. He wore a smirk on his face as he watched her remove another finger from her mouth and lick it off. She'd never thought there was anything provocative about sucking Cheeto residue off her fingers. She did it all the time. But the look on Luke's face made her rethink it. She quickly stopped and rubbed her hands on the back of her shorts. Luke quietly laughed.

"Well, ladies, aren't you a sight to be seen?" said Clay, leering at them.

An odd array of swimwear, sportswear, sleepwear, and grunge, they were a sight to behold. It was so dramatically opposite of opening night, when they'd been gussied up in their designer gowns and pushup bras. Tami was in her element. Ashley would have sworn she somehow knew about the surprise. Tami stood with hips thrust forward in a pose that made every other part of her look perfect too. The cameramen could barely keep their cameras or eyes off her.

Gwen stood next to Tami. Her lower lip quivered, her eyes glassy and ready to tear. Her long, pale blond hair framed a face devoid of color. Without expertly applied makeup, her long lashes were all but transparent. Her natural eye color of light gray was a shocking difference from her usual look of contact-tinted big baby blues surrounded by dark lashes and eyeliner. Normally, Gwen's eyes popped. Today they were barely noticeable.

Ashley struggled to prepare her game face. Normally she gave a lot of thought to her approach for each ceremony and how she would play it to her benefit and advantage—mainly to get kicked off. Now her only hope of getting axed was the lack of time she and Luke had spent together and, maybe, how horrible she currently appeared in her natural state. After all, they'd only had the ski date and a few chance meetings. Not enough time to make a good, solid impression.

She did want off the show, but it was difficult not to get caught up in the excitement and fun. She wouldn't mind another kiss from Luke. She felt so confused. What did she want?

Luke looked each of them over, as if trying to make the selections quickly in his mind. Ashley didn't envy him his position. Cutting four of them with no time to prepare was a huge endeavor.

Clay looked smug now that he was no longer in danger of physical harm. "Ladies, thank you for your cooperation in this impromptu rose ceremony. Luke, you may begin." Clay stepped off to the side and out of sight.

Luke took one rose from the basket and held it between his thumb and forefinger, gently twirling it as he stood thinking.

"Before I begin, I want to take a moment to let you know I am as surprised by this as you are." He scanned the ragtag cast of contestants. "I'm not ready to do this. I'm not prepared to send four of you home. I haven't had the opportunity to get to know some of you as well as I wanted to." He made eye contact with each girl as he shared his feelings.

"As a quarterback, I'm used to making surprise decisions in a clutch, so that's what we're going to do here today. I don't mean to hurt anyone. Obviously you aren't ready either. If I had my way, I wouldn't send any of you home, but that's not an option. So let's get this over with."

Ashley was relieved he felt rushed. She might finally get her wish to go home. A twinge of regret fluttered in her gut, but it would be a relief to escape the constant vigil of the cameras catching her every bad move. She refused to believe the butterflies could have anything to do with Luke. After all, she wasn't interested in him.

He began calling names one by one. Kate. Cricket. Tami. Rachel. While the ecstatic four huddled to the side in quiet euphoria, Luke paused to look over the remaining six. Two would stay; four would go. Shelby was poised in her beach wrap, looking her gorgeous beauty queen self. Natural Meg stood calmly, surrounded with positive energy to guide his decision. Jenny the snuggler gazed cozily up at him as she batted her baby blues. Gwen trembled, eyes wide. Next to Ashley stood Liz, tall and beautiful. Ashley waited. Luke knew she didn't want him. He knew she didn't like him—at least, not very much. She held her breath.

Looking over the remaining six, Luke picked up another rose. "Ashley."

Her breath came out in a huge sigh. So that was it. She was in again. What was his problem? She stepped forward and accepted the rose.

"Thank you," she said, trying not to glare at him.

As she began to step away, he stopped her. "Wait." He reached up to her forehead to wipe something off. "You have Cheeto marks on your forehead. Orange isn't your color." A dimple appeared on his cheek.

"Great. Thanks." She was beyond embarrassed. This whole morning was a hideous experience.

Then Clay stepped up next to Luke. With all the seriousness he could muster, as though it were brain surgery or at least the final round of the Masters, he said, "And now for the last rose." *Moron.*

Luke gave the remaining women one last look and pushed his hand through his hair, giving it a disheveled look. He took a deep breath. "Jenny."

Ashley and Rachel quickly turned to Liz, who was in the reject group. Their overcrowded bedroom would feel empty without her. Liz looked disappointed, but not shattered. She gave them a reluctant wave good-bye and blew them a kiss after mouthing "Good luck! And call me!" Then she said her good-bye to Luke.

Gwen, on the other hand, was a mess. She did the ugly gulping-for-breath cry. Her normally porcelain face was red and splotchy with emotion. Luke hugged her as she sobbed, rubbing her back to calm her down. His shirt was all wet when she finally released him. Fortunately, there was no makeup to smear.

After Liz and the others left, the celebration party felt strange. Ashley was subdued as she tried to digest the events happening around her. The game was getting out-of-hand and she didn't know how to stop it. Why did Luke keep her here? This was the third rose ceremony, and they'd only shared one group date together. Granted, it included a stolen kiss that lifted her so high she could have flown off the chairlift. But it didn't mean anything. Heck, Liz had so much more going for her than Ashley did. Why did life make what you wanted so hard to get, while what you didn't want literally banged down your door? She had all but told him off. Okay, maybe she actually had told him off. She didn't want to waste any more time on this stupid show.

What was she going to do? She had no idea how to take charge of this out-of-control situation and make it work for her. She was stranded for at least another three days or so. *Crud.*

As Ashley carried empty glasses from their impromptu celebration into the kitchen, Rachel came up behind her.

"What are you doing?"

Having no idea what she was talking about, Ashley replied, "Clearing glasses out of the great room?"

Eyes narrowed, Rachel snarled, "That's not what I meant, and you know it. What's your game?" She stood, hands on hips. "You've been saying all along that he's not your type and you don't care that much about the show, and yet you keep manipulating your way through each stage."

Ashley moved to the sink and set down the glasses. *Whoa, where's this coming from?* She turned around and leaned against the sink.

"This was your plan from the beginning, wasn't it?" Rachel accused. "Everybody's got their game plan and yours was to play hard-to-get." She paced back and forth in front of Ashley, then stopped and pointed a finger in her face.

Ashley braced herself against the counter. She needed some leverage as she heard Rachel's accusations.

"You played Liz and me for a couple of fools. You walked in the door with a big story about tripping on the sidewalk and how embarrassed you were. Bull!

You fell down in front of him so he'd have to notice you." She started pacing again. "You wanted to chum up to us so you could sail through more easily."

Ashley stepped away from the counter and reached out to Rachel. "I haven't done anything. He picked me. I didn't pick him."

"This is the first time I've ever been in love and you're trying to ruin it."

"Oh, Rach, don't say that." Ashley stepped forward. "You don't even know him. It's been less than two weeks. You think you're in love, but this is all artificial. It's not real."

Pulling away, Rachel argued back, "Yes, it is." Pain etched her face.

"Honey, I don't want to see you get hurt."

"I thought you were my friend, but you used me from the moment we met."

"No, I didn't."

Rachel took another step back. "Yes, you did, but it's over. He's not going to fall for you. What I feel is real, and nothing you do can change it. I feel it, and I know he does too."

Rachel turned and left the room, and Ashley stood dumbfounded and alone. Alone except for the cameraman lurking in the corner, filming the whole exchange. She hung her head in frustration.

Life just turned from bad to worse. She didn't know what to do or how to make it better. She hoped that Rachel would calm down and that they'd be able to talk it through later. Ashley left the kitchen and the despised camera behind. She moved through the great room and up to her bedroom. Tami leaned against the doorway with an evil gleam in her eyes. She had obviously overheard and was gloating at the discord between the two roommates.

When she reached their bedroom, Ashley saw the empty closet and the cleaned-off dressers. Rachel had packed up her belongings and moved in with one of the others. Ashley sat on her narrow bed and felt as desolate as the room looked. What had once been an overcrowded room filled with clothing and laughter was now just a vacant space with a lonely, hollow feeling.

She lay back on the bed and stared at the ceiling, too deflated to get cleaned up. The only good thing about the whole, sordid experience had been her friendships with Liz and Rachel, and now they were both gone.

How many times in life would she find herself misunderstood, alone, and miserable? Obviously too many.

She knew that she should quit the pity party, but the idea of jumping back into the thick of things with no emotional support felt all but impossible.

She needed to get off this horrible show.

Luke stood under the hot shower, steam filling the room, the walls pressing in around him. The hot water beat against his back, pounding in the memories of the morning. He couldn't stop thinking about the heartbroken looks on the faces of the women he'd sent home. It hurt.

The foggy air was suffocating. *Why is this bugging me? I don't care about them. I've dumped women before. Maybe because it's on TV and the world will see it?*

He leaned his arms against the glossy wall before him, resting his head against the cool marble as the stream of guilt continued to roll over him. Have I always hurt women this much? Is this my legacy? Why haven't I ever committed before?

This was supposed to be fun. It was crazy and chaotic, and the women were beautiful and entertaining. But here he was dumping someone every couple of days. The similarities to his life were only too clear. Why was he always dumping women?

This game was hitting a little too close to home, and he wasn't sure he even wanted to keep playing it, much less to win it.

Chapter Eight

"**M**ail call."

Ashley looked up from her comfortable chair on the back patio where she could see the turquoise colors of the ocean. She sat, legs curled beneath her, and read another of her trashy novels, this one with a bare-chested Viking on the cover. The catalpa tree threw off dappled shade and her ever-present can of diet cola sat on the table.

"Ashley, where are you?"

Jenny's squeals of excitement filtered back from the front of the mansion—date mail had arrived again.

"I'm coming." She uncurled herself from the chair. Time to join the chaos inside.

"Hurry up, Jenny's ripping the envelope open."

"Don't get your undies in a bundle, I'm on my way."

Ashley left the quiet peace of the patio to join the growing group in the great room. There was always excitement when date mail arrived. An unspoken competition existed among the ladies to be the one to find it and share the good fortune with the lucky date recipients. While Ashley couldn't care less about finding the mail, she was curious to know about the next big date and who it included.

With only six bachelorettes left, the stakes were high. Her strategy to play it quiet in order to get voted off had obviously failed. But as much as she needed to job hunt, she admitted she enjoyed the downtime. She read constantly, blasting through her books, sleeping late, and getting a little color while hanging out in the Southern California sun. And her being included in so few activities had kept the camera crews away from her most of the time. All in all, things had gone pretty well, which meant she was due for another date soon.

Jenny proudly waved the card in the air with a squeal. "It's a group golf date! And three get to go!"

"Who's going?" Tami demanded, her voice snippy. She took the card from Jenny. "Let me read it." She stood back to formally reveal the contents of the card.

There will be lots of sun, but don't wear
  your suit,
'cause water is a hazard and sand just won't do.
We'll be surrounded by grass, but aim for the tee.
Go grab your clubs and come play with me.

We will pick you up early. You don't need a ticket.
Today is for Ashley, Tami, and Cricket.

A smug expression came over Tami's face, as if she'd known all along that she'd be picked. Her air of confidence and haughtiness always fascinated everyone. Rachel looked crushed. She turned her sullen face away from them and left the room.

Kate, however, seemed genuinely happy for Cricket, as was Ashley. Cricket was a pretty, quiet girl who always came off as a little shy but very sweet. Ashley liked what little she knew of her. She seemed smart and well-grounded underneath her model-like body and short, sassy hair.

There were high fives and hoots of congratulations for the date winners. Ashley was pleased to have another opportunity to get out of the mansion, even if it meant going on a date. Another group date! Plus, she was curious to see how things went between her and Luke.

But golf? Ashley had played golf a couple of times with friends years ago, and once with one of her boyfriends, but she had no true interest in the game and had never developed any skill. More times than not, she'd whiff the ball when she swung. Was whiff a golf term, or had she made it up? She would wind up, concentrate, aim at the ball and whiff right over the top. So humiliating. She'd look like she was going to nail the ball and then, poof! All that action for nothing. Ugh.

Her best experiences had been when she'd golfed with girlfriends. When they hit a bad ball, they would hit another one, or pick it up and throw it closer to the hole. Ashley hoped tomorrow would be similar.

The limo picked them up promptly at seven the next morning. Luke was ready and waiting at the course.

"Wow, does he look hot!" Tami said, with a hungry look.

Ashley couldn't argue. He stood at the front of the clubhouse dressed in tan shorts and a brilliant white golf shirt with a Whistling Straits logo. The fine fabric of the shirt rippled over his muscular shoulders. His arms, legs, and face were tanned. Obviously Luke spent a lot of time outdoors. He stood taller with his golf shoes on, looking casual and comfortable. He was in his element.

Luke helped them out of the limo and greeted each of them warmly with a kiss on the cheek. Not a bad way to start the morning. Ashley put a hand to her cheek as she stepped away. They were ushered into the pro shop and fitted with clubs and shoes. Each of them wore their own version of appropriate golf attire. Ashley wore tan Dockers shorts and a black sleeveless top with a collar. Her hair was pulled back in a pony-tail and she wore a simple black visor.

Tami was an entirely different story. She wore fitted white micro shorts which showed off her gorgeous long legs. Of course . . . she was all legs. Her top was a hot pink stretchy tank top that molded to her everywhere. The low V-neck nicely displayed her generous assets. She wore her thick, dark hair down, sported a classy pair of designer sunglasses, and had a smile that shimmered with rose-colored gloss on her full lips. She looked like a million bucks. She also looked like she belonged on a photo shoot, not a golf course. Luke's gaze, as well as those of the cameramen and country club staff, roved over Tami at every opportunity.

Cricket, on the other hand, looked like she'd walked off the cover of some preppy golf magazine. She moved confidently around the pro shop wearing black pleated shorts with a classy peach sleeveless golf shirt and a cute little coordinating visor. As she turned an educated eye to select a putter, a golf glove hung out of her back pocket.

Cricket was a golfer.

Ashley felt the pit in her stomach grow.

Outside, two golf carts sat ready. One held a large black golf bag strapped on the back. Tami edged in next to Luke. "I hope you don't mind if I ride in your cart. I could use a few pointers."

Ashley could have pointed out a few things to her, but didn't waste her breath.

After hitting a couple of practice balls at the golf range, Ashley didn't feel any better. Luckily she'd hit most of the balls off the tees, but none had gone very far. She hopped in the cart next to Cricket and tried to drum up some courage.

Cricket looked over at her. "You don't golf much, do you?"

"That obvious?"

"Let me just say you could use a few tips."

"I need a lot more than tips. How about a body double who golfs? *That* would be helpful."

"Oh, don't worry. You'll be fine," Cricket assured her. "I don't want to offer help where it's not wanted, but I think if you correct just a few things you'll be able to hit the ball better."

"Really?" Ashley asked skeptically. "You think you could do something to improve my dismal skills?" She looked at the huge course laid out before her. "I am so bad at this game. Why couldn't I have gone to a baseball game, or to the zoo or something?"

Cricket smiled in sympathy. "Don't worry. After we tee off, I'll stick by you and we'll see what we can do to get your ball in the air."

"Thank you. Anything you could do to help would be appreciated. I'll pay you back somehow. I'll even rub your feet. You get me through this horror of cameras filming every embarrassing swing and I'll be your new best friend."

"No problem. I'm glad to help, and you don't need to rub my feet," she said and laughed.

They arrived at the first tee. Luke stepped up to take his first shot. After sinking the tee deep into the dense grass, he stood back and took a couple of practice swings. Luke moved with such fluidity. His eyes focused somewhere down the fairway as he stepped up to his ball, his stance totally relaxed as he wound up and swung. Luke hit the ball with such precision and force that it flew high into the air and seemed to glide forever before popping down not far from the green.

Amazing. Ashley had never seen a golf ball hit so beautifully or so far before. Not that she'd had much opportunity. The ex-boyfriends she'd golfed with were not very good. In fact, next to Luke, they were total losers.

Luke invited the ladies to hit. Tami sauntered right up and bent down with her tight little butt in the air and placed her ball on a tee.

What a sleaze.

When she hit the ball, there was a nice little loft to it that Ashley would have died for. But then, she'd love to have a figure like Tami's too.

Cricket stepped up and tried a couple of practice swings. When she hit the ball it was grace in motion. Ashley heard a nice little "ping" as her club hit the ball and it soared high into the air and straight down the fairway. Beautiful.

"Your turn," Luke prodded Ashley when she didn't move to the tee box.

"Oh yeah, right." She tried to approach the tee box with confidence and set her ball and tee in the grass, and sighed. She searched for some real courage, but the damned camera was focused on her—waiting.

Suddenly turning to the others, she leaned on her

club. "Listen you guys, I am *so* not a golfer. I mean, I'm not even good at minigolf."

"Not a problem," Luke reassured her. "We're just here to have fun. No pressure." He offered her a warm smile.

Fun. Just here to have fun.

She focused on the ball and took a deep breath in an attempt to relax.

Yup, just have fun.

She took another deep breath.

Okay, now you're stalling. Just hit the dumb ball.

She wound up and swung, trying to keep her eye on the ball and not the group gathered to watch her tee off. Her club came around, and by some miracle hit the ball. Her euphoria was short-lived as the ball took a forty-five degree turn to the right. At least it went a somewhat respectable distance.

Ashley picked up her tee and walked over to the group. She glanced at Luke. "Yeah, that was really fun." A smile curled at the edge of his mouth.

Back in the golf cart, Ashley and Cricket were able to go the opposite direction of Luke and Tami.

"Okay, just shoot me now. Put me out of my misery."

"Oh come on, you were fine. Don't be so hard on yourself."

"Easy for you to say. You golf like the club is an extension of your arm. What's with that? Where did you learn to golf?"

Hesitating, Cricket replied, "Well, I grew up a country club kid. We spent our summers at the club swimming, golfing, and playing tennis."

Perfect, how could she not have guessed? Cricket, always impeccably dressed and displaying perfect manners. The girl was bred to play good golf. Unlike Ashley, who was born to embarrass herself. If there was one thing Ashley had, it was humility. Lots of it. How could you not when you screwed up as much as she did?

Approaching the next ball, Ashley said, "Okay, Country Club, I beg you, help me survive this miserable day." They smiled at each other and walked up to her ball where Ashley received her first lesson. Cricket walked her through every shot. She taught her how to properly hold the club and where her feet should be planted.

She still wasn't golfing well, but at least she seemed to hit the ball more often and accurately.

Across the fairway, Tami worked Luke at every opportunity.

Watching Tami's performance made Ashley ill. She and Cricket would look at each other and roll their eyes as Tami batted hers at Luke and laughed at every amusing thing he said.

It felt that their date was more like a twosome than a foursome.

After six holes, Luke approached. "Hey Ashley, how about we switch off and you join me for a while?"

"I don't know if that's such a good idea." Her pulse began to race.

He walked over to her cart and removed her golf bag. "And why would that be?"

"You've seen me golf. I'm terrible," she said, following after him "And I happen to know good golfers hate to play with bad golfers. I don't want to cramp your style."

He lowered his sunglasses enough to gaze over the top at her. "Don't worry—I'd never let you do that." With a quick wink, he turned and walked away with her bag.

Ashley stood, mouth open and cheeks scarlet.

Tami pouted her way into the cart with Cricket. Ashley climbed into Luke's cart. He appeared unaffected as he grinned at her. "Ready or not, here we go."

The cart flew forward and Ashley put her foot up on the side to keep herself in place. Apparently Luke liked it fast—at least when driving.

Golfing together wasn't quite as horrible as she'd thought it would be. While her drives were short, she hit pretty straight, and Luke's constant banter kept her entertained. Each time he hit the ball, Ashley couldn't help but watch in awe. There was such power in his swing. His muscular arms gripped the club gently and his whole body wound up and then released in one smooth, awesome swing. His athletic physique was a beautiful combination of strength and grace. She wondered how it would feel to be held in his arms.

"Are you this good at every game?" she asked.

Leaning toward her, he gazed into her eyes. "Oh yeah, I can play any game you want. What'd you have in mind?"

Torn between wanting to know what those games might be and smacking him for his provocative comment, Ashley settled for giving him a stern look and she walked around to get back in the cart. "Sports, Luke. I'm talking about sports. I asked if you're good at all sports."

Pulling forward to drive toward Ashley's ball, Luke responded. "I love pretty much any sport with a ball—baseball, tennis, soccer, golf," he gestured to the breathtaking course around them.

"And football," she added.

"That one's my favorite," he said. "I also enjoy fishing and trap shooting. Basically anything that gets me outside is a winner."

"So, are you bad at anything?" she wondered aloud.

"Well, let's see." He thought. "I'm not the best at some, but I don't embarrass myself either."

"Unlike me," she pointed out as he pulled the cart up to her ball and she hopped out.

"I wasn't talking about you."

"Right," she said, grabbing a club. "Who else is here embarrassing themselves on the golf course? You know, I just don't get it. How is it you're so good at everything you do? You play just about every sport, you're pretty smart for a dumb jock, and you're good-looking. It's not fair."

The moment the words were out of her mouth she regretted them. Why feed his ego when it was obvious that he was far more confident than anyone she'd ever known?

Not missing the opportunity, he replied, "You think I'm good-looking?" The smirk returned.

She'd love to wipe it off, maybe with her golf club. She tried to hide her flushed face as she prepared to hit her ball.

"No, really." He refused to let the subject go, the irritating man. "You said I was good-looking. I thought I wasn't your type, that you were immune to all my charms." He leaned in close to her.

"Oh, you are priceless, not to mention full of yourself!" Ashley swung the club and nailed the ball, sending it a respectable distance down the fairway for the first time.

"Not bad," he said, admiring her best shot of the day. "You should golf with attitude more often. Anyway, you're the one who started it with the good-looking comment. To be honest, I've been wanting to talk to you again. I'd like to get to the bottom of this thing about me not being your type."

"Here we go again."

"How do you know I'm not your type when you

hardly know me? Shoot, we've barely spent any time together. How can you make such a quick judgment about someone you don't know?"

"That's an excellent point," she agreed, hoping to change the subject as she climbed back into the golf cart to avoid the approaching cameraman. "You don't know *me*. So why have you kept me in this game when I've only been on one group date with you? You've spent a lot more time with some of the others."

"True," he said as he pulled away, "but did it occur to you that maybe I know who I'm interested in and I'm just trying to give the others a final chance to show their best colors?"

"Right," she replied, skeptical but also a bit wary. This was not the answer she'd hoped for. He made it sound as though he was interested in her. "You know," Ashley said, glancing back to make sure the camera cart wasn't within earshot, "if it were me in your place, I'd ditch the ones I have no chemistry with first."

"Is that right?"

"Then I'd get rid of all the money grubbers. You don't want to keep any gold diggers hanging around to get their hooks into you. Do you?"

"Excellent point," Luke agreed, which encouraged Ashley to continue as he drove slower. The cameras couldn't catch their conversation while they were moving.

"Good. Then you need to get rid of the annoying

ones, the ones with irritating habits." She quickly glanced up at him as she jabbered on. "Bad laughs, body odor, and people who babble on and never shut up."

"So, what's your point?"

"My point," she said, turning toward him in exasperation, "is that you're doing it all wrong."

"Am I?"

"Yes. First of all, you've kept the biggest gold digger I've ever met."

He eyed her doubtfully.

"You've kept some of the most annoying people to walk the face of the earth. Don't you notice how Kate can't make a move without batting her baby blues?" Ashley mimicked her by tossing her head around and batting her eyes constantly. "Tami can't get near you without flashing her cleavage or bending over." She glared at him pointedly.

Luke laughed.

"And Jenny, yuck. All she does is hang on you and pet you like you're a lap dog. Doesn't it drive you crazy? I'd go nuts. Give me some breathing room. Who would want to be smothered like that? Especially someone like you. I'd think you would cherish your private space."

Luke smiled as he pulled up next to her ball. He was amazed at her accurate descriptions of all the women and her awareness of his need for privacy, not to mention the fact that she could talk incessantly and not miss a beat.

"But then again, you are known as a bit of a Romeo." She stepped out of the cart and grabbed a club. "You probably love all the groping and warm bodies pressed against you all the time."

"Oh, sounds like you're jealous," he taunted, hoping he'd hit the mark.

"Jealous? Oh please. I know when I'm out of my league, and believe me"—she lined up to hit—"I am so far out of my league I don't even know how to play the game." She swung and nailed the ball for the second time that day.

Luke watched her ball loft through the air and land on the green. He turned to Ashley in amazement. "What makes you think you're out of your league?"

"Well, for starters, I don't fit into the mold here." She gestured to Tami and Cricket in the distance. "Everyone here is known for their beauty, their smarts, their money, their sports ability, and their hot bodies. I don't fit into any of those boxes. I am the average girl. Plain Jane all the way." She tossed back her ponytail and pushed the flyaway hair out of her face.

"Then what are you doing here?" He admired her feisty attitude and natural beauty. She was unflawed by the trappings the others seemed to want and need.

"Yes, I am still here, and it's your fault," she accused as she neatly dodged the question about why she'd been chosen for the show. "How about we make a deal?"

"A deal?"

"Yes," she answered. "I'm out of here next round."

"Hmm, I'll have to think about it. What's in it for me?"

"What do you mean, what's in it for you?"

"You get to go home, so what do I get?"

"What do you want?" she asked suspiciously.

He tilted his head to the side and raised his eyebrows. "What do you want to give me?" he whispered in a low, suggestive voice.

She slapped at him with her golf glove. "You are such a pig!"

"I know," he said in a devilish voice as he guided the cart along the fairway.

She slapped at him again with her glove. Luke laughed and grabbed the soft glove. She started to poke him in the sides and pinch at his arm. Now Ashley laughed too.

Suddenly Luke looked up and realized he was about to drive right into a sand trap. He swerved the cart tightly to the left, effectively throwing Ashley out of the cart and into the bunker. She tumbled through the sand, losing her visor, and ended up sitting and sputtering sand out of her mouth. Sand covered her everywhere.

The camera cart behind them caught the swerve and toss perfectly, forever preserving it on film.

Luke stood next to the golf cart and laughed at her sitting in the sand. Ashley glared, looking like she was about to chew him out, when she saw the cameraman closing in. She immediately closed her mouth and stood up as unceremoniously as possible and climbed back into the cart.

"Let's go," she said, staring straight ahead.

"Sorry about that. Are you okay?" He tried to swallow a laugh. "Look, you've got sand in your hair." He reached over to gently brush it away.

"Let's go," Ashley demanded, her eyes pleading as she pushed his hand away.

Luke glanced at her and then at the cameraman, realization dawning. He nodded. "You're embarrassed because they caught you flying through the air."

"I'm not embarrassed," she whispered. "Please, let's go now. Please."

He moved the cart away from the cameras. "Hey, I'm sorry. I didn't mean to throw you out back there, and I sure didn't want to embarrass you."

"I told you, I'm not embarrassed. I just don't like cameras watching my every move." She sat back, rigid.

He cocked his head and looked at her in bewilderment. "Well, then, this is a pretty dumb place to be if you don't like cameras."

"That's an understatement," she said softly.

Luke was floored. Moments before she had been relaxed and carefree, laughing openly, bantering with him and flirting. Something had flipped a switch on her. She'd transformed into someone he'd never seen before. Something was going on and he intended to find out what.

"So, what's your problem with the camera?" he said as he pulled up to the green.

Ashley quickly hopped out of the cart, selected her putter and walked onto the green. The camera cart pulled up and focused on Ashley's uncomfortable posture. She stood with her back to the camera and looked out across the course.

As Luke pondered Ashley's odd behavior, Tami and Cricket came flying up in their cart, Tami hooting and hollering as she drove.

"Did you see my shot?"

Luke turned to see Tami literally leap out of the cart and run over.

"Look how close I am. It was only my third shot!" She ran over to Luke and jumped up and down in a blatant attempt to get him to hug her.

Luke put a hand on her shoulder and stepped back. "Nice. Sorry I missed it." He glanced at Ashley and saw her begin to relax with the cameras focused on Tami. "Okay, Tami, let's make sure you read the green correctly and make this shot."

Tami followed Luke to the other side to look at the grade of the green and decide the best way to hit the ball. The cameras followed them.

The next hole was a par five. Tall grass lined one side of the fairway. Like a magnet, it pulled Ashley's ball right into the thick of it. Luke immediately hopped into the cart. "Let's go find the ball."

Ashley still appeared a bit shy after the cameras had caught her falling out of the cart, but she no longer looked panicked.

"There is no way we'll find the ball in those tall weeds."

"Don't be so sure. I've got a pretty good eye for things that go missing." He smiled warmly at her. "I watched your ball and I have an idea where it might be." Luke reached over and patted her reassuringly on the leg.

He pulled the cart up to the edge of the tall grass. "Okay, here's where it gets fun. Grab your wedge. It's the only thing that'll get it out of here." He was already out of the cart and walking slowly through the grass looking for the small white ball.

Ashley followed behind with her club. "Isn't there some rule about how long you can look for a lost ball?"

"So the girl does know golf." Luke grinned up at her. "Yes, as a matter of fact there is. It's five minutes."

"I hate to spoil your fun, but I'm sure we've been searching for at least that long."

"Nonsense." Luke was unaffected by the tall weeds that scratched against his legs. "Where's your sense of adventure, your positive attitude?"

"I left both of those back in the limo," she said under her breath.

Luke laughed as he quietly pulled a ball from his pocket and dropped it into the grass.

"Aha! Found it!"

"You've got to be kidding." She struggled over to him, fighting weeds along the way. "Unbelievable." She looked around at all the tall grass. "Nice job, Sherlock. So, how am I going to get it out of here?" It was at least twenty feet to the mowed portion of the course. She stared intently at the ball and nodded to herself. "I think the best bet is to pick it up and throw it."

Luke laughed. "No, you can't. That," he said as he sternly pointed a finger at her, "would be cheating. And we don't cheat."

"Maybe you don't cheat, but I definitely do, especially in situations like this." She stood stubbornly with her hands on her hips, staring at him with a look of challenge.

"No you don't." Her attempt to look difficult and mean amused him. "It won't be that hard. I'll help you. First we'll push down all the weeds around the ball so you have plenty of room to swing."

Together, they stomped over the weeds to create a small clearing around the ball, scratching their legs as they went.

"Good," he said, assessing the area as though about to perform surgery. "Now approach the ball and get a feel for the pressure you'll need to hit it out."

Ashley raised an eyebrow at him and followed his directions. "I am now approaching the ball." She walked cautiously up to the ball talking to it as she went. "Okay, I'm in. Ball, we need to get you out of here safely. What's the plan? Do you feel pressure? What pressure do I need to hit you out of here?" She peeked over her shoulder at Luke. "Oh, you want me to pick you up and throw you?" She bent down to pick up the ball, and Luke grabbed her gently by the arm. The touch of his warm grasp went straight through her whole body.

"Oh no you don't. You're going to hit it fair and square." He let go of her arm and she felt suddenly chilled. He took the golfer stance. "You're going to bend at the knees a little more than usual and you're not going to take a big swing. You're going to swing with your wrists only." He demonstrated it for her. "Then the ball will pop into the air and up and over the grass."

She gave him a blank stare.

"You can do it. Just have a little confidence."

Ashley lined up next to the ball and bounced at the knees a couple times. She stepped forward, staring intently at the ball, and bit her lower lip. Luke watched with a mix of appreciation and amusement. He saw that she was trying very hard to get the shot. She was so cute in her intensity.

She took a deep breath and swung. The club connected, but at the wrong angle and speed. The ball popped up about four inches and settled back into the weeds.

Ashley turned to Luke. "I told you so." She tossed her

club down and stood with her arms crossed and hip out.
Luke bit the inside of his cheek to keep from grinning.

"It's not funny."

"No, it's not." He struggled to keep a straight face.
"But you are."

Ashley grinned.

"Okay, come here." He picked up the fallen club
and motioned her to stand in front of him before the
ball. She stood before the slightly relocated ball and
glanced back at him. He handed her the club. "Now
show me how you grip the club."

She held the club in the standard golf grip.

"No, for a wedge you want to hold it like this." He
tried to move her hands on the club, but she flinched
and then shook her hand out. He eyed her skeptically,
then reached out and took her right hand in his. He
turned it over and discovered blisters developing on
her palm and fingers.

"Ouch! No wonder you're having trouble." He gently
caressed her sore hand, examining it as he went. "Why
didn't you tell me you had blisters?" He tenderly held
her raw hand in his large warm grasp. "You've been
gripping the club way too hard." His finger lightly traced
each blister. Goose bumps appeared up her arm. It was
no surprise to him she hadn't complained. While she
whined about her ability to hit the ball, she wouldn't
complain that she was hurt. "You're supposed to hold
the club as though it were a baby bird."

"A baby bird?"

"Yes," he said. "A baby bird. Here, I'll help you get this ball out of here."

He turned her back toward the ball and stood with his arms wrapped around her like a warm cocoon. He leaned down to hold the club with her. Her silky hair brushed against his cheek as he repositioned himself around her.

"Hold your hands like this." He moved her hands higher on the club and closer together. He placed his hands over hers, enjoying the softness of her skin. "Now, we're going to swing using only your wrists, not your arms." He slowly guided her through the feel of the swing until she did it right.

"Okay, now remember to keep your grip relaxed. This time we're going to hit the ball together. Ready?" Holding her in his arms felt too good, much nicer than Tami, who used every opportunity to make a move on him. Ashley just fit.

"Ready?"

He detected the concentration in her voice. She was really trying, even though she didn't have a clue about what she was doing.

Together, they swung the club from their wrists and hit the ball squarely. It popped up into the air and sailed over the grass, back onto the fairway.

"We did it!" she said turning in his arms to look at him.

"Yes, we did."

He wanted to lean down and kiss her right there,

surrounded by weeds. But he knew the cameras were catching every word, every move. Tami and Cricket were in their cart, waiting. There would be an audience. He knew it was not what Ashley wanted.

When he kissed her again, he wanted it to be for them alone.

Chapter Nine

"This is getting so hard, Kelli." Ashley sat on the edge of her bed, head in hand, and spoke quietly into the cell phone. The bedroom door was closed and locked.

"What's happening?"

"Last night they sent three home. Three."

"They're wasting no time. Who went?"

"Jenny, Kate, and Rachel." Ashley hurt inside when she thought of losing Rachel's friendship over this debacle of a game.

"But you're still in?"

"Yes," she sighed in resignation.

"How do you feel about that?"

"Gosh, I don't know. Confused more than anything, I guess."

"Talk, honey. I've got all the time in the world."

Ashley stood and walked over to the open balcony door. She stared out into the distance, unable to focus on any one thing. "You know how much I've hated this. Well, at some point it started to be fun. I found two great friends in Liz and Rachel. Or I should say I *had* two great friends. I don't know anymore. I'm pretty sure Rachel hates me. She thinks I was playing them to get closer to Luke."

"If only she knew the truth."

"No kidding. And now spending time with Luke . . ." She paused, trying to pinpoint how she really felt about him. "He's growing on me. Nice guy, sensitive and smart, great sense of humor. And easy on the eyes."

"Of course."

"Kelli, I think I'm crushing on him." She smiled to herself, embarrassed.

"Oh really?"

"Okay, yes, I have a big, stupid, annoying crush."

"Hey you, listen up. He's a great guy and you've been put in a position where you're supposed to like him. It would be odd not to."

"You think so?"

"Definitely. Don't beat yourself up. Go with the flow."

"All right, but Kelli, I'm in the final three. This is getting scary."

"Don't let yourself go there. Take it one day at a

time and live in the moment. That's who you are. Stay true to yourself. Okay?"

"Okay."

"Now, what's up next?"

"You're not going to believe this." Ashley paced the length of the room.

"Tell me."

"We're going on overnight dates!"

"Where are you going?"

She stopped pacing. "Costa Rica, baby! Hiking in the rain forest!"

"Yes! This gig isn't looking so bad right now, is it?"

"Not bad at all."

Chapter Ten

"Whatever you do, don't look down. When you're ready, go ahead and jump."

Oh yikes! How do I always get myself into these things?

Ashley used all the courage she could muster. She chewed on her lower lip as she looked into the distance, trying to put a lid on her fears. It wasn't working. Her palms were sweaty and her knees shook. Each second seemed like minutes.

Okay, it's now or never. She took a big breath, jumped off the platform, and screamed louder than she ever had in her life.

The free fall seemed like it lasted for several minutes, although in reality it was only a second or two before the cable leveled out and she flew along the zip line high over the rain forest. Ashley's screams turned from terror to delight as she relaxed and began to enjoy the breathtaking experience of gliding over the lush greenery of Costa Rica. The zip line was three hundred feet above the valley floor and almost a quarter-mile long. She felt like a bird soaring over the trees. Far below, the foliage of the giant plants and trees appeared as tiny as houseplants. The rushing river was a tiny trickle of water.

After a couple of minutes, Ashley approached the next platform and the end of the line. She squeezed her gloved hand on the cable as she'd been instructed to do, and her speed slowed down in time for the guide to reach out and pull her up onto the platform.

"Whew! That was amazing," she said to the Costa Rican guide. *"Muy bien."*

He quickly unhooked her safety strap from the zip-line cable and rehooked her to the security line on the tree platform.

She heard hooting and hollering, and turned to watch Luke sail high over the abyss she'd just traversed. He flew quickly toward her, his approach fast. Too fast.

"Luke, brake! You're coming too fast!

"Brake, brake," yelled the guide, holding his hands up in the position taught to them minutes before.

At the last possible moment, Luke squeezed his gloves tightly on the cable and jerked to a stop right at the safety catch, causing him to swing wildly.

"What a rush!"

The guide pulled him to the platform and rehooked his safety strap to the tree.

Luke held on to Ashley. "Wasn't that awesome?"

"I was scared at first, and then it was wonderful. I couldn't believe how high we were. I was actually looking down on the birds flying below me."

"I know. How about the speed? I had no idea we'd be going so fast."

"Do we get more? I want to do it again."

"You bet. There's about a dozen zip lines."

They spent the next hour and a half riding one zip line after another. Each line began from a tall tree on the top of a hill and went over a valley below. The cameraman alternated filming their takeoff or their landing at the platform. He either went before them or filmed them as they went by. Ashley didn't even notice him anymore. The experience was exhilarating, like nothing Ashley had ever experienced before. This was something she'd shared only with Luke, just the two of them. After finishing the last ride they removed their harnesses and safety gear.

"I've never dreamed of doing such a thing! In fact, I never even knew something like this existed," Ashley said.

"Doesn't it make you feel like you could do anything now?" Their eyes met and held as they shared the excitement.

"Sure does. Bring it on!"

"What'd you have in mind?"

"I don't know—bungee jumping, river rafting, maybe mountain climbing." Heck, she'd fly to the moon if it meant Luke would do it with her. Now, where had that thought come from?

"Down, girl. I think we've created a monster."

"What's next?"

"Let's go check with Jim."

They walked over to the producer. He was saying good-bye to the canopy tour guides.

"So, what's up next?" Luke asked.

"Well, as soon as we get you some gear, we should be ready to go. We'll be hiking deeper into the forest to where camp is already set up and waiting for you. It's a beautiful hike, and it should take about two hours to get there. It takes four hours by car. I can't wait for you to see it. The spot is spectacular." Jim handed each of them a backpack. "Everyone carries a small pack of provisions in case anything unexpected happens along the way."

Ashley bubbled with anticipation. Sharing these new experiences with Luke made them even better. She couldn't wait for the rest of the day to unfold. They exchanged smiles, eager to continue on.

What a gorgeous sight! Ashley couldn't remember the last time she'd been surrounded by such natural beauty. It no longer rained, and the plants and grass grew lush and green. The raindrops dripping from the leaves and the wet forest floor made everything smell fresh.

Most of the production team had been left behind, not to mention the catty women and the stress of house life.

This was definitely paradise.

They'd hiked for about half an hour when the path became slippery and treacherous, thanks in part to the recent rains. As Ashley navigated around a small crevice, she heard Roger, the cameraman, swear. The rest of the group turned to see as he sat on the wet path with a grimace, holding his knee in pain.

Luke ran back and kneeled next to him. "Let me take a look."

The producer, Jim, took the heavy camera strap off Roger's shoulder and carefully placed the equipment to the side.

More colorful words came out of Roger's mouth as Luke expertly examined his knee and gently applied pressure to check the extent of the injury.

"What do you think, Doctor?" Ashley asked, peering over his shoulder.

"I'm not an expert, but I'd bet my lunch you've got a sprained ACL."

"Do you think you can walk, or are we going to have to carry you out of here?" asked Jim.

"I don't know. Let's give it a try," answered the wiry-looking cameraman.

Together, Luke and Jim helped him to his feet. He gingerly put weight on the injured leg.

"So far so good," he offered.

"Try a small step," Luke instructed.

Roger took small, tender steps. When he turned to come back, though, he cringed in pain.

"We see this kind of injury a lot during games. As long as you don't pivot or turn on it, you should be able to get around."

"What are we going to do?" Ashley asked, worried about the future of the date.

"Looks like we'll have to scrap the hike and head back to the trailhead," Jim said. "We can catch a ride when the next canopy tour comes through."

"Does that mean the whole date is over?" Ashley asked, devastated. The day had been going so well and she hated to see it end this way.

"No, no. Once we get Roger checked out, we'll reschedule. Maybe we can start again tomorrow. In fact, there's a back road we can drive to get into camp in the morning. Takes a while, but it'll work."

Luke stepped forward. "I agree. Roger needs to get his knee looked at as soon as possible. However, I don't think it's necessary to reschedule the rest of the day. It's taken us hours to get this far, and I know he captured some great footage of the zip lines."

Roger nodded.

"Why don't Ashley and I hike ahead to camp? Jim, you can carry the camera while Roger hobbles back to the trailhead. It shouldn't take long. The only thing you'll be missing is our arrival at camp and we can re-film that in the morning. No one will ever know."

Ashley loved the idea. They could enjoy their time together without anyone watching every move they made or listening to every word they said. She crossed her fingers behind her back.

"I don't think that's a good idea, Luke," Jim answered. "The whole point of being here is to get it on film."

"No, the whole point of being here is for Ashley and me to have an extended date with time to get to know each other. It's been great so far, but I don't want to put the skids on now and try to fake our way through it tomorrow. It's not fair to her or to me. Plus, the other overnight dates didn't have to be resched-uled."

Ashley looked from Luke to Jim and back again. It was hard to tell if Luke was gaining ground or not.

"Well, I don't think it's a wise idea."

"Listen, Jim, I've been flexible through all the shenanigans and last-minute surprises. I'm going to have to insist we stay on-schedul. Sorry to be diffi-cult, but this is how it's going to be."

Ashley held her breath. Jim eyed Luke, then Ashley and then Roger.

"All right. I'm not pleased about it, but I'll let it go your way."

"Good choice."

Ashley couldn't detect any excitement in Luke's

voice, but he did reach over and squeeze her hand tightly.

"The setup team will be gone, but you should have everything you need. There is no cell service here. On second thought, if one of you gets hurt—"

"Jim! I can handle this." Irritation rang strong in Luke's voice. "Do you want us to hike back with you?" he offered.

"Okay. What do you say, Roger? Could you use some help?"

Roger continued to walk slowly, testing his leg. "No, I think it'll be okay. Like you said, it's only a problem when I twist or turn. So I guess I won't do that."

"Are you sure?" Ashley asked with true concern.

"I'll be fine. You go enjoy the rest of the day." Roger winked at her.

She thanked him with a big smile.

"Watch your step." The path became steeper and was slick with wet leaves over a thin layer of mud.

"I've got it." Ashley reached out and grabbed a tree as she stepped around a large boulder. "It's a good thing Roger didn't take this hike. I don't know how he would have done it with a heavy camera."

"No kidding. It's not exactly for the faint of heart."

A gentle breeze kept them cool under the midday sun as they made their way along the trail. Ashley was content to walk in peace. The terrain gradually grew more rugged and the climb became more difficult.

"Take a look at that drop-off!" Luke pointed.

"Holy moly, I'd hate to fall off that."

"No kidding. Here, take my hand."

Ashley placed her hand in Luke's. He carefully guided her over a narrow stretch where the path was nearly washed away.

"Are you sure this is the trail?"

"I think so." Luke scanned the area. His gaze continued down the path and focused on a break in the plants and trees. "There it is." He pointed ahead to a spot where the trail leveled off and widened up again.

Ashley stepped with care and stood next to Luke. "I see it now." Her eyes followed the path backward to where they stood. "Luke, I think we have a little problem. A section of the trail is missing."

"I see what you mean."

"How are we going to get across?"

"Very carefully. Follow me." He took her hand in his and led the way over the slick, narrow path until they came to where part of the trail had literally slid down the side of the hill and out of sight. The break in the path was about two and a half feet wide. On the left was a deep ravine. On the right, the hill climbed sharply with a natural spring flowing down the side to where the path had washed away.

"What do you think?" Ashley studied the break.

"We jump over."

"Yeah?"

"Yeah." He raised his eyebrows at her in challenge. "No guts, no glory."

"Hmm." She examined the path ahead, or the lack thereof, trying to locate the best place to land after she jumped over the small crevice. "Okay. Let's go." She stepped past him.

"Wait a minute. I'll go first."

"I want to go first."

Luke crossed his arms over his chest and pierced her with a steady gaze, as if judging her ability to make the jump.

"You've led the whole way. It's my turn. Besides, you said 'no guts, no glory.' I've got guts and I want glory." She grinned at him.

"Fine, go ahead." He motioned with his hand.

"Good." She concentrated on the small leap she needed to make. As she was about to jump—

"Remember, no guts, no glory."

She froze in place. "Stop that. You startled me!"

"Sorry. You need any help up there—in the lead?"

She gave him the evil eye. "No, I don't. Now would you shut up?"

"Sure, I just thought you should—"

Ashley concentrated on the other side and took a running start. After five quick steps she jumped and landed easily on the other side. She turned back to Luke and laughed. "Piece of cake."

Her laugh became a scream as the path fell away, taking her with it.

Chapter Eleven

Luke ran to the spot where the path fell away. He searched over the edge, panicked. His heart pounded in his chest.

"Ashley! Ashley! Where are you?"

Silence filled the air. Even the birds made no sound.

He scanned the foliage for a glimpse of her blond hair.

"Ashley!" he yelled louder. Luke's panic grew with each second. He studied the steep slope inch by inch. The dense foliage made it difficult to see anything. Dirt that was once a part of the path had disappeared down the side of the ravine. He crouched on the ground to get a better view below.

"Ashley!" he shouted again, feeling more desperate.

"Luke?" Her voice sounded frightened.

A wave of relief washed over him. "Ashley, are you okay?"

"I think so."

"Where are you?"

"I'm down here."

Luke thumped his head against the ground a couple of times and laughed. "I know you're down there, but where? I can't see you."

"On the side of this hill, I imagine."

Another wave of relief crashed over him. "Can you climb up?"

"I don't know. I'll try."

Luke tried to spot her as she climbed with no success. After a long minute, he broke the silence. "How's it going?"

"Pretty good, and you?"

"Ashley, are you making any progress?"

"A little. It's really slippery and there's mud everywhere."

"Can you dig in with your fingers and the toes of your shoes?"

"I'm trying."

Luke waited. He willed her up the side. Not seeing her was killing him.

"Luke?"

He tried to follow the sound of her voice. "Yes."

"I broke a nail."

"Listen, smart aleck, concentrate on what you're doing. I can't help you get up here if I can't see you."

"Men. You always get mad when you're not in control."

"Ashley?"

"Yeah."

"Shut up and move it."

"Fine, but I still say— Aaaah!!!!"

"Ashley?"

There was silence. Luke stood up, ready to climb down after her.

"Luke?"

Her voice sounded small and scared again. Relieved, he stood with his hands on his knees, head down. "Are you okay?"

"I think I'm going to need your help to get out of here. I slid farther down."

"Don't worry. Sit tight and I'll figure something out. Do you have any idea if you're on my side of the path or on the side you landed on after you jumped?"

"Umm. Hang on. I see you! Luke, I can see you!"

"Wiggle the plants around you." He scanned the side again, praying he'd see the telltale signs of leaves moving. He spotted a small tree waving. "I see you too! Don't move."

Her face looked small and vulnerable from where he stood. She was about fifteen feet below him. He examined the crevice. It was now almost five feet across. Luke backed up several steps, and without hesitating ran at full speed. He planted his foot and leaped across the open expanse. He landed on the other side and hugged the wall to his right to ensure that he didn't follow Ashley over the side.

"Did you jump across?"

"Yeah."

There was a moment of silence.

"Show-off."

"Listen up. I want you to look around and describe the area to me. What are you holding on to and where are your feet? Is there a landing you can get to?"

Luke removed his backpack and looked to see if there was anything useful inside.

"Well, let's see. There are big green plants everywhere. I'm holding on to the roots of one."

He pulled out two water bottles, a bag of gorp mix, bug repellant, matches, a jack knife, and sunscreen.

"It looks like there are a bunch of rocks higher up near you."

"Yeah, what else?" He reached farther into the pack and found a small first aid kit, a flashlight and, thank you, a rope.

"Well, it's pretty steep."

"What are you standing on?" He quickly unwound the rope to check the length. He guessed it was about twenty feet.

"A tree. Actually, it's a little tree."

He raised his head. "What do you mean? You're standing on a tree?"

"Kind of. This little tree is sticking out of the hill, and I'm standing on the base of its trunk."

"What's below the tree?"

She sounded fine, though the description of her location did not sound good. "Nothing. It's, um, a drop-off."

"Ashley, don't move. I've got a rope." A sheen of perspiration covered him. A heavy weight settled on his chest, and his heart was beating in overtime. He had to get her out of there.

"No, I'm pretty much staying right here. Not going anywhere."

"Good. Now I need you to wiggle the plant again so I can find you. Be very careful." He watched and, sure enough, he saw leaves shake. Her face peeked out pale and worried. "I see you," he yelled down to her.

"I see you too." From her precarious perch, Ashley gave him a strained smile.

"I'm going to throw this rope down. See if you can catch it." He rolled up the bulk of it and tossed it to her, only to have it become hung up on some foliage. He tried a few more times, but each time it landed out of her reach.

"Luke?"

"Yeah, Ash?"

"I thought you were a quarterback. Shouldn't you be able to throw the rope right to me?"

"Well, yes." He pulled it back up. "In a perfect world I would, but this rope isn't a football and *you* are not a receiver."

"Come on, big guy. Suck it up and get me the rope."

He threw again. This time the rope landed on the leaves of the plant she held on to. "How's that?"

He could just catch her saying, "About time." Obviously her fear wasn't great enough to squelch her attitude.

"Listen up. I want you to wrap the rope around your waist and tie it. Can you do that?"

"You bet your sweet feet I can. Hang on a sec."

He held the other end of the clothesline-like rope.

"Okay. I did it, but I'm not sure the knot is going to work. I wasn't a Boy Scout and they didn't teach rope tying in Brownies."

"Can you wrap it around your arm too? That should help." He gave her a minute to maneuver. "Are you ready?" he asked, impatient, wanting her back by his side, safe and sound.

"Ready."

"Great. Now hang on. I'm going to pull you up slowly. Hold on tight to the rope with both hands and use your feet to dig in and climb as I pull. Try to get some leverage to keep yourself moving. Here we go." Luke wrapped the rope around his right hand several times and pulled it taut. He pulled it slow and steady inch by inch. "How're you doing?"

"Okay." Anxiety edged her voice.

"Hang on. I'm going to reposition and pull harder." He placed his feet against a large boulder at the top of the slope. The tension of the rope burned his hands.

"You still okay?" She was about halfway up.

"Yup," she groaned.

He continued to pull the rope hand-over-hand. He felt the muscles in his arms and shoulders bulge with the strain. His panic changed into steely determination. He would get her back safely and she would be fine. He would accept nothing less.

"Stop! Stop, stop, stop!"

"What? What's wrong? Are you okay?" He held Ashley and the rope in place, gripping tightly.

"I can't hang on. The rope is biting into my hand and I need to move it. Loosen it up a little. I'm braced against a rock."

Luke stole a glance over the side and saw her clinging to the rocky side less than four feet below. Her face wore a pained look as she wound the rope around her arms and hand once again. Jagged rocks spiked the remaining distance between them.

"Okay, I'm ready."

Luke readjusted his grip and began a steady pull to get her the rest of the way up. He heard Ashley groan as she slid over the rough terrain. Suddenly, she was only an arm's length away.

"Look up, Ash. I can reach you." He grabbed her hand, rope and all. With the solid feel of her warm hand in his grasp, a weight of worry lifted off him. He breathed a huge sigh of relief. One more strong pull and she was up over the side and tight against him as he lay down on the ground, his arms firmly around her. After a secure, bone-jarring hug, he held her away to get a good look.

"Hey, what's this?" Tears filled her eyes and she shook all over. He put his hand beneath her head, weaving his fingers through her hair. He turned her face to him. "What's going on?"

Tears slid down her cheeks. She pushed them away with her arm. "The rope was slipping. I thought I would fall and . . ."

"There was no way I would have let you fall." Thankful to have her safely back with him, he pulled her into his arms and cradled her. She released a deep, shuddering breath. Her body relaxed in his arms.

Without realizing what he was doing, Luke leaned forward and kissed her lips tenderly. As he lifted his mouth away from hers, he heard her soft intake of breath.

He leaned in for a deeper kiss, enjoying the softness of her mouth. The way she returned the tentative kiss melted his heart. Her hair spilled through his fingers as he held her, and he brushed his other hand against her jaw as the kiss deepened. He slowly pulled back. Her eyes fluttered open.

"Oh," she softly exhaled as if awakening from a dream.

He was in heaven.

Luke came to his senses. Reluctantly, he lifted his

head and gazed into her glistening eyes. He watched as she returned from the faraway place to which she had gone.

"Girl, you are driving me crazy."

"What?" She slowly focused on him.

He smiled at her confusion. "Nothing. Let's take a look at you and inventory the damage."

Luke sat back on his knees and checked for injuries. Red marks wound around Ashley's arm from the pull of the rope. He hadn't realized how close she'd been to losing hold. Her knuckles were scraped and raw from rubbing against the side of the rocks. He turned her hands over and saw the underside of her arms, scratched and skinned. He frowned. His heart went out to her as he realized how painful her rescue had been. She'd acted so strong. He reached out to inspect her right hand, but she pulled it away and cradled it to her side.

"I landed on it when I fell."

"It's okay—let me see." He reached again, and this time she allowed him to inspect it. He gently ran his fingers up and down the length of her arm. Her skin was soft and smooth to his touch. Other than being a bit dirty and slightly scraped, it appeared to be all right. He cupped his hands around her injured one as if willing it to heal. After a few moments, he raised it to his lips and kissed it lightly. "All better now?"

"All better." She smiled back.

He finished his examination, and noticed her knees

and shins were also battered and covered with blood and scrapes. "You don't look so good." He ran his fingertips lightly up and down both her legs. "You took quite a beating. I don't think your legs are going to look too good in shorts for a while, not to mention a swimsuit."

She scrutinized her legs. "I think you may be right. However"—there was optimism in her voice—"this may actually be a good thing. There are so many scrapes, I have that much less leg to shave. My morning shower will go so much faster."

Luke shook his head. No matter what happened, her spirit couldn't be broken. She was once again running at the mouth. Smart aleck.

"Well, if you think you're able to walk . . ." He stood up and extended a hand to help her up. "I think we should move out of here. Let's try to find this jungle paradise they told us about."

"Sounds good to me." He helped her to her feet and they returned to their expedition.

In less than thirty minutes the terrain became easier to hike and they began the descent into a small valley. They both breathed a sigh of relief when they reached a spot overlooking a clearing filled with all the amenities one would expect for the king of a small country.

"I believe we've found the promised land." Luke led the way down the hill to the haven below.

A white silk tent sat off to the side of the clearing

near the base of a beautiful rock wall with vines and plants growing out of it. The sides of the tent were made of sheer netting, pulled open dramatically to reveal the centerpiece, a large bed made up with satin linens and large comfy pillows in varying sizes.

They exchanged uncomfortable glances. Each managed to keep a straight face. Barely.

Fresh flowers accented the tent. Red rose petals were scattered on top of the bedspread. Each side of the tent featured a comfortable chair and a stand, on which hung a white linen robe. A table with a pitcher of water and a basin, as well as stacks of fluffy white towels and bars of sweet smelling soap, sat to the side.

Together they walked across the clearing toward two chaise lounges covered in a soft ivory fabric with a table between them. The table was set with candles and wine glasses, and the chairs overlooked a small waterfall a mere fifty feet away. The water cascaded down the rocks and fell gracefully into a pool below, surrounded by a bed of mossy grass. Another stack of towels sat on a rock near the pool.

"Wow, this is amazing," Ashley said as she walked over to a round table set for dinner. An ivory tablecloth covered it, and a beautiful centerpiece filled with large exotic flowers and greens from the rain forest graced the center. Two tall white tapers waited to be lit.

"Luke, look what I found."

A few feet from the table, partially hidden by several plants, sat a large rattan picnic basket and two coolers.

"I'm still admiring camp, and here you're all excited over food."

"What? I'm hungry." She opened the coolers to see what feast was hidden within.

"Me too," he whispered under his breath as he watched her explore.

Ashley sat on a chaise lounge eating tender chicken off a skewer.

"Hey, Luke." She wiped her fingers on a napkin and reached for her glass of red wine.

"Yeah?"

"What's it like?"

"What?" He sat back, relaxed, a nearly empty beer bottle cradled comfortably in his hand. He rolled his head toward her.

"Football. What you do."

"You want to know what playing football is like?"

"We've spent the whole day together and I'm curious. There's so much I don't know about you. What's it like living a life where you get so much media attention all the time? How do you play football when you have five cameras following your every move? They catch everything you do, even when you scratch yourself or pick your nose."

Luke chuckled.

"No, really, people criticize every move you make. Everything you do right or wrong is critiqued and discussed over and over on TV, on the radio, and in newspapers. It would drive me crazy! I couldn't stand it."

"Hmm. That's an interesting question."

He wondered if he should give her the short version, which usually satisfied curious fans and media interviewers, or give her the real answer. Tell her how frustrating it was to be criticized for mistakes when the blame often lay with the guy who was supposed to catch the ball, but ran the wrong way. Or to have your character chewed apart like you were some media darling in Hollywood.

On the other hand, it was better than any life he could have imagined. He was living his dream. He loved playing the game, being in charge of things, making the all-important comeback in the final two minutes. It was the most exhilarating life he could imagine. He'd experienced so many highs he could die a happy man.

Then again, some of the baggage that came with it was a real drag. But hey, when you were paid as well as he was, how could anyone complain? The general public didn't understand. They only saw dollar signs, fame and fortune. No complaining allowed, which was fine with him.

"It's all part of the job. It's my responsibility to be accessible to the press and to be under everyone's scrutiny. I would be disappointed if it were otherwise."

"You can't be serious. You expect to be treated that way?"

"That's pretty much how this game works. You play well, you get coverage. You play rotten and you get more coverage. The press loves to get sound clips when you're down."

"I couldn't stand it." Ashley moved to the coolers as she spoke. "It's all I can do to put up with the cameras on this reality show. It goes against everything that's normal. Who in their right mind would expect that as a part of their life?"

Luke watched as she fished around in the cooler and pulled out two more plates of food.

"In fact, to be honest, it nearly kills me every time I see one of those stupid cameras facing my direction. I want to tell them off, or smear something on the lens. I know these guys are doing their job, but I hate it. I really hate it." She set down a tray of chocolates between them, along with more shrimp and strawberries.

"Really? Now that surprises me."

"It does?" She handed him another shrimp. "Why?"

"Thanks." He tipped his shrimp toward her. "Because you appear comfortable being yourself. You always speak your mind and don't seem to buy into all the competition of the game."

"Uh-oh, am I that obvious?"

"You're not obvious, just yourself. I can tell it's the

real you, probably more than anyone else here. Whenever I see you, you're doing whatever you want, the way you want to do it. You don't sugarcoat things or suck up like everyone else. You don't care what anyone else thinks."

"I have been awful."

"Not at all."

"I really didn't want to stand out. I wanted to blend in and be myself. I can't get into this fake girly thing. Doesn't it drive you crazy having all these women fawning over you all the time?"

He gave her a cockeyed look.

She laughed. "Okay, don't answer. I know. You're in heaven. Who wouldn't want a bunch of gorgeous women hanging on your every word and telling you everything you think you want to hear?"

Luke sat back thoughtfully. "Actually," he said, "I am tired of it all." Hesitant to bare his soul, he reached over for another large shrimp.

"Yeah? Go on."

He realized he trusted Ashley and wanted to share his thoughts with her. "At first I was a nobody. No one cared about Luke Townsend. I was a young kid having fun doing my thing, getting into trouble. Partying too much, acting young and stupid. And then everything began to fall into place and it seemed like overnight I was the greatest thing in football." He took a bite of the shrimp. "I've spent my life playing football. When I was little, I used to practice signing my autograph so that one day, when I became famous, I'd have it down perfect."

"Amazing. You've wanted this since you were a kid and you got your dream. Do you realize how few people can say that? I'd say all your practice paid off. Don't you make ten dollars every time you sign your name? Do you even own rights to your own signature anymore?"

"Yes, I still have rights to my own signature. Want my autograph? I'll give it to you—for free."

"Ooo, the great Luke Townsend offers me his autograph. Thanks, but I think I'll pass. I'm not much into autographs. Or into the rich and famous, for that matter."

Faking a hurt look, Luke threw his shrimp tail at her. "I am so offended." She picked it off her top and threw it back.

"I've never known anyone to turn me down. Are you aware how much you could make with it on eBay?" Not very much, he thought to himself. There were thousands of Luke Townsend autographed items out there. He was definitely overexposed.

Ashley shook her head and rolled her eyes. "You are way too confident. You really need to be knocked down to size."

"Knock away, baby," he said with an evil grin.

"Yeah, right." She took another sip from her glass instead. "So, go on."

"Well, suddenly I attracted all kinds of media attention and started to have a huge fan following. It seemed no matter where I went, people were waiting for me. People wanting to buy me drinks, shake my hand, hang out, or . . . whatever." He hesitated, trying to find the right words.

Everything was free, no strings attached. "It's amazing how many doors are open to you when you're at the top."

Luke drained his beer. "On the other hand," he said, "your life is under a magnifying glass. You think you have secrets and then you read them in the morning paper. Or worse, a reporter asks a very personal question in front of a room full of media. Something you thought was private and sacred is suddenly on the ten o'clock news. It's the pits. And then it gets back to your family. At first I thought my family would never know about my wild activities or speeding tickets, but it all finds its way to them. Everything."

"Life in the spotlight doesn't sound very appealing."

"You know what else I hate?" he asked, not waiting for an answer. "I hate the way we go into a game injured. Half the team is banged up and barely able to get out of bed in the morning. We go out there and put every ounce of energy we have into the game. We get beat up, thrown to the ground, bashed upside the head. You try to hide the concussion you think you have and not walk with a limp." Luke passed his empty bottle from one hand to the other like a football.

"Then the press jumps all over you about why you threw a certain pass, or why you ran the ball instead of kicking a field goal. You give it your absolute best, and you can barely drag yourself off the field at the end of the day, and then you have to face stupid questions after the game. And you know what else?"

Ashley shook her head.

"You have to treat the reporters with respect, because if you answer their stupid questions with idiotic answers, they'll edit it together to make you look like a fool. They can take anything a person says and turn it around so you appear like an uneducated, back-hills moron."

"I had no idea. You always seem in such perfect control out there. I don't know how you do it. If it were me they were hounding, I'd crawl under a rock until they left. I'd never read another paper or turn on the TV again."

"Well, I must admit I don't read any of the local sports pages. It's great to read the good stuff, but the bad doesn't benefit me. Trust me, I know when I don't play well. I don't need the newspaper to tell me."

"See, this is another reason why you and I could never be together. I hate it when the media gets too personal, nosing into people's private business." Ashley shrugged and picked up a strawberry, rolling it between her fingers as she spoke. "I could never rise above it and say the right things. I would blow. It would be ugly and nasty and embarrassing. People would know my inner secrets. Ugh. How awful. I don't know how you do it."

"I have pretty thick skin. It doesn't hurt that my dad

was tough on us growing up, and my brother never lets me take myself too seriously. He keeps me down to earth and gives me regular reality checks." He looked at Ashley closely. "But why in the world are you here if you dislike the media? Don't you realize how much PR they're going to do when this show hits the air?"

Ashley stared at him. "I never thought about that. Are you sure?" she said with her mouth full.

Luke saw dread wash over her. "I haven't looked ahead at the schedule, but I assume it's all part of the contract. Media tours, all that stuff."

"Oh great. That's just fine." She took a gulp of wine and looked off into the distance. "Shoot me now."

"You want to elaborate on that?"

"Well, if that stupid camera was here right now, I wouldn't be saying any of this."

Luke nodded in understanding.

"How can I explain?" She reached for a large piece of chocolate. "I'm a really private person. Don't get me wrong. I have lots of great friends and I love to have fun, but I don't want my life broadcast to anyone other than my closest confidants." She took a bite of the chocolate. "Let me say—being on this show was a bit of a . . . surprise . . . a last-minute decision. I guess you could say I am stretching myself here. I'm not used to putting myself out in front of people like this, especially not a television audience." Ashley hesitated and then took another bite. "Once I got on the show and met you . . . no offense, but I knew we weren't a good fit."

Luke regarded her skeptically. He didn't buy her story for a minute. Chemistry spoke louder than words.

"Well, there was this mob of gorgeous, skinny women surrounding you at every turn. I knew there was no way I could compete with any of them, and quite honestly, I don't want to."

Luke laughed, recalling the golf outing and how determined she had been despite her obvious lack of skill. Apparently she didn't realize how hard she tried to be competitive.

Ashley continued. "I am not interested in fighting for someone. Those women don't know anything about you, and yet they throw themselves all over you and claim to be in love. It's such a joke. You don't fall in love with someone in three days. It's a big game, and I guess I don't play games well." She popped another large piece of chocolate into her mouth.

"Well then, how did you get so far in this one?"

"It's a mystery to me," she answered, her mouth full of chocolate. "My plan was to fly under the radar and get out of here quick. I had no intention of hanging around to see what it was all about. But *you*," she said and pointed her finger at him. "You messed up my whole plan by giving me those dumb roses. I even asked you not to. So *you* tell *me*. Why are you keeping me here when you know I'm not interested?"

Luke stared at her and watched color rush to her face. Their kiss on the side of the ledge had indicated that she was very interested. And so was he. He hadn't felt that kind of heat from a kiss in a very long time, and he'd bet Ashley hadn't either.

"Okay, let me get this straight. You entered a reality game you don't believe in. You decided I was a loser and you wanted out. So you tried to . . . What was it? 'Fly under the radar' so you could get off the show. And now that I've kept you here this long and selected you for this fabulous date, you tell me you aren't even a little bit interested?"

He laid on the guilt very well. Somehow he knew Ashley would never hurt his feelings. For all her sarcastic wit, she didn't have a malicious bone in her body, unlike many of her competitors whom he had already sent away.

"It's not that I'm not *interested* in you." She fumbled for words. "It's just—I don't feel that you're my type. And I'm certainly not yours."

"Whoa, don't go putting words into my mouth. Now you're beginning to act like the media."

"Sorry, but we're very different people. You're a public person and I'm a private one. Considering your line of work, I don't see how it could work. It's nothing personal."

"It's business," he quickly interjected.

"Something like that." She smiled. "Listen, I really do enjoy your company, so let's make the best of this adventure. Hey, we lost our cameraman and producer. The world is our oyster and ours to explore. Let's see what else this paradise has to offer."

You are the pearl in the oyster. He narrowed his eyes at her. "Bet you can't get to the waterfall before me," he said.

"Bet you I can." She leaned toward him.

"Prove it." His eyes fixed on hers in challenge.

"Fine. On the count of three. One . . . two . . . Oh, look!" She popped up and pointed back to camp. "The camera crew's back."

Luke swung around, startled and disappointed, only to hear Ashley say, "Three!"

Chapter Twelve

Ashley knocked her plate to the ground as she took off running.

Luke pounced after her like a wildcat pursuing its prey.

She ran as fast as she could, letting out little shrieks as she heard Luke coming up behind her. Her heart pounded. She dodged small plants and rocks as she went. Ahead lay the waterfall. Behind her, Luke leaped over obstacles with the agile grace of a true athlete. Right before she reached the pool of the waterfall, Luke was on her. He snatched her around the waist and swung her away from it.

"No, no, no," she squealed. "I was almost there."

His strong arms held her firmly in place. Ashley's

legs kicked and swung as she tried to get down, but he'd have none of it.

"You little cheater!" His breath warmed her neck.

"Put me down," she demanded, laughing. His solid chest pressed tight to her back, and his firm arms against her sent tingles down her arms.

"You're not getting off that easy." He lifted her up higher, tossed her in the air and readjusted his hold. He now held her cradled to him with her legs over his arm.

"Stop it!" she squealed.

"Cheaters must be punished."

Ashley fixed him with her meanest glare. "Don't even think about it."

He walked toward the pool of water.

"Don't you dare!" She squirmed in his iron grip. "Luke, I'm serious. Put me down." She pounded against his chest. "This isn't funny," she said, trying not to laugh.

He pretended to trip and faked a fall, leaving her momentarily suspended in air before he caught her. She screamed, then started to laugh and put one arm around his neck to hold on.

"You scream like a little girl—did you know that?"

"Well, you're a bully—did you know that?" Ashley's heart beat faster.

He walked to the edge of the pool and pretended to toss her in. She tightened her hold around his neck. He held her easily against him.

"Well, well, well. What are we going to do about this?" He looked first at her, with a glint in his eye, and then at the water. He shuddered for effect.

Ashley tried a stubborn don't-you-dare-do-it expression.

"Seems to me there's more than one way to skin a cat," he said, as though trying to decide what to do.

"Put me down. Over there," she quickly added, pointing to the side where there was a carpet of soft grass. "Remember, I'm hurt. I've been through a traumatic experience."

He ignored her. "The way I see it, we can do this fast or we can do it slow." He grinned. "I'd prefer fast, 'cause you're getting kind of heavy." He stepped into the water one step at a time.

"Brrr. Nothing like fresh mountain water."

"Please." She looked at him pleadingly, hoping the sweet-and-polite thing would work. She let go of his neck to show him her wrist. "I don't want to ruin my watch."

"You are so lame." Her watch was smashed with broken hands. "Time's up!" Luke launched her so fast, she had no chance to hold on. *So this is what it must feel like to be a football shot down the field.* She barely had time to scream before she plunged into the pool.

Water filled her open mouth.

She came up sputtering, hair covering her face. "It's warm!" she choked out in delighted surprise. "The water is warm!"

Luke grinned.

"You knew!" She stood up, her clothes drenched and clinging. She pushed the hair out of her face as she stepped forward, then slipped and fell back into the warm water. "You are such a jerk!" Ashley splashed warm water at him.

Luke removed his shirt, entered the pool, and swam out beyond her to deeper water. "Pretty awesome, don't you think?"

He stole the words right out of her mouth. She didn't think she could have spoken anyway. Seeing him bare chested in such close proximity took her breath away.

They floated around as he shared what the producers had told him about the natural hot spring. An active volcano several miles away heated the ground-water throughout the region. This was one of several natural hot springs in the area. And it was their private paradise for a few hours.

The warm water caressed her skin and felt decadent. "There must be special minerals in the water that make it so soft and pure." It felt like nature's kiss upon her skin.

They played in the water, floating on their backs and gazing up through the overgrown vegetation at the dimming sky. They swam under the waterfall and let the hot water beat against their weary muscles. Ashley found a natural shelf off to the side where she sat and relaxed, letting the water do its magic. The sound of water cascading over the rocks proved hypnotic.

Water sluiced over Luke's sculpted muscles. He

seemed unaware of the beauty of his body or its effect on her.

Ashley lifted handfuls of water and let it run through her fingers.

Luke swam over and sat next to her on the cozy ledge. After a few minutes of relaxed silence, he said, "I have to say I don't think I've ever heard a girl scream as much as you."

Ashley sent a small splash his way. "Hey, so I'm not a tomboy, I'm not athletic, and I'm not competitive. I guess you could say I'm a girlie girl. Except that I don't look like one."

"You look better than most of the girls from the show."

Zing. "The last time a guy chased me like that was in kindergarten when we played 'Catch 'Em and Kiss 'Em' on the playground." She skimmed her hand over the top of the water letting it run between her splayed fingers. Being chased by the boys gave her a special feeling in her stomach even back then. She felt it now with Luke.

"Did they ever catch you?"

"Once in a while." She smiled, remembering back. "It was always Gerald Newton who caught me."

"Gerald, for a five-year-old? He sounds like a winner."

"You don't know the half of it." She pictured the short little guy in his starched white button-up shirt.

"He wore a crew cut on his round head, and thick black glasses."

"You're making it up."

"No, honest. It's the truth. He was a nerd." She looked up with a grin. "I guess that's where my love of nerdy men started, way back in kindergarten." Ashley continued to let the water run through her fingers and watched it splash into the pool.

"So, what would Gerald the nerd do when he caught you?"

"He'd push me up against the bricks of the school wall and give me a hard peck on the lips."

Moving closer, Luke placed an arm on each side of her and held onto the rock shelf. "*I* caught you. Does that mean I get my kiss?"

Ashley squirmed. Luke's kisses were as soft as the enchanting water. He was like a drug she was becoming more addicted to every day. Her head took over and she responded, "I don't think that's such a good idea."

"I think it's a great idea. We're in this beautiful setting. There's no one else around. You don't have to worry about being caught on-camera, at least for a few more hours." The low timbre of his voice was spellbinding.

"But Luke . . ." A flush of warmth heated her skin.

"Shush." He put his finger against her lips. "If you let Gerald kiss you in the school yard in front of everyone, it's only fair that you let me kiss you here in paradise where no one can see us."

He had a point there. If she ever wanted to really enjoy kissing Luke, this might be her only chance.

He slowly took his finger away and replaced it with his lips in a gentle, sensual kiss.

Ashley didn't bother fighting it. Her insides turned to jelly. He rested his hands on the embankment behind her as he slowly kissed her senseless. How could a body be so relaxed and yet so tightly strung at the same time?

"Come here." Oblivious to everything around her, Ashley let him lead her into slightly deeper water where they could stand or float. He gently touched her face. Tracing the outline of her chin with his finger, he slowly moved to her cheek and back again. Each touch awakened more nerve endings. He took her into his arms and recaptured her mouth. Ashley's pulse quickened.

Chapter Thirteen

A rose is coming my way, and I'm actually excited. Who would've thought?

"You sure look content," Cricket commented. She took a seat in a cushioned deck chair next to Ashley's.

"Is it that obvious?" All she could think about was her time alone with Luke. The experience had left her a changed woman.

"Yes."

Ashley noticed Cricket wore a big smile as well. "Looks like you enjoyed your getaway too."

"I did. They taught us how to sail on our trip up the coast. What an amazing boat. Luke is so much fun. He kept me laughing the whole time."

"He does have the gift, doesn't he?" A warm glow grew inside Ashley whenever she thought about Luke.

They sat on the back deck and shared stories as they waited for the producer to give them the heads up for the next rose ceremony. The air felt warm and fresh as the sun began to set.

"Aren't you a couple of peas in a pod?" Tami sauntered onto the deck, hips swaying. "I hate to break it to you girls, but one of you is going home tonight." Tami plopped down into a lounger. "After our night in South Beach, baby, he's all mine. In fact, you can both go home tonight."

Ashley and Cricket raised an eyebrow at each other. "Is that right?" Ashley knew it wouldn't take much to get Tami to spill the beans.

"I had the man wrapped around my little finger." She waved her pinky at them.

"Where's South Beach?" Ashley asked.

Tami repositioned her dress to better display her shapely tan legs. "Miami, you idiot. You really are a country bumpkin, aren't you? It's the hottest place in the U.S. All the top models and A-list stars go there. It's *the* place to be seen. In fact, I wouldn't be surprised if we make the cover of *Star*."

Ashley shrugged her shoulders. How was she supposed to know about South Beach? She knew State Street in Madison, and even Rush Street in Chicago.

"Did I mention the white sand beach?" Tami continued. "Let me tell you, after one application of suntan oil, he was all mine." She fanned herself.

"So you had a good time?" Cricket asked.

"Good doesn't even touch it."

"What did you do when he wasn't polishing you with suntan oil?" Listening to Tami talk about Luke made Ashley's stomach sour. Her time with him was so special, it was impossible to believe Tami's could have been as well. At least she hoped not. Prayed not.

"Well, after our afternoon by the ocean, did I tell you that we strolled the beach? He wore those amazing swim trunks, showcasing his six-pack in all its blessed glory. I swear every woman on the beach watched him. But he was all mine," she said. "I wore my gold suit. We stopped traffic. We put all those starving models and big, strong firemen to shame.

"Later, we hit the boutiques. I made sure those snotty sales girls knew exactly who they were dealing with. Once they knew I had the NFL MVP on my tail, they gave us the red-carpet treatment. It's so nice to be with a celebrity."

Ashley and Cricket exchanged looks again. Tami certainly had an ego.

"Anyway, we ended up at Nikki Beach." She looked at Ashley. "You have heard of Nikki Beach, haven't you?" Ashley shook her head. "You are so pathetic!" Tami continued without pause. "It's the hottest night spot in South Beach. It's on the beach, obviously, and instead of tables and chairs, everything is white beds and pillows. I spent the entire night with Luke. Dancing and talking. The poor sot wants me so bad he can't see straight." Tami ran her long fingernails up and down her arms. Her goose bumps were visible from where Ashley sat.

"My word, but you're shallow!" Ashley exclaimed.

"What? He's eating right out of my hand. I can make him to do anything I want. I have the power. I want his money and he wants me."

"You don't know him very well, do you?" Ashley asked.

"Well enough. He's a jock and needs to be told what to do." She stood up. "All's fair in love and war." She flashed an evil smile and strutted back into the mansion.

Ashley threw her hands in the air. "Why do I let that woman bait me? I fall for it every time."

"It's her gift. Don't let her get to you. She's so full of herself, she wouldn't know love if it bit her on the behind."

"She does make you doubt his feelings, though," Ashley added.

"Yeah. I was feeling pretty special until Tami showed up. Now I don't know. Let's hope for the best. If Tami is who he really wants, he deserves her."

"I'll second that." Tami's innuendoes had rattled Ashley, but she'd done her best to block them out. Tami was a troublemaker and nothing more. She hoped.

Compared to the first night, the great room seemed cavernous. The trio stood in a small group in front of Luke, waiting. With cameras in place, a silent tension filled the room. Ashley's anxiety caused every muscle in her body to tense.

Up until that point she'd only wanted to get off the show and go home. Now she wanted desperately to stay and be with Luke. The time they had spent together in Costa Rica had deeply affected her. They'd clicked and she didn't want it to end. She didn't want to believe Tami. Luke couldn't be working both of them, or all three of them for that matter. Could he? She hated the doubt that crept in.

Luke's gaze slowly moved from Ashley, to Tami, and then to Cricket. He gave each of them a warm and reassuring smile. He reached into the basket and pulled out the first of two roses. He looked at each of them again and then said, "Cricket."

Damn, why couldn't he call her first? The rat. But Ashley was glad to see the blond girl move on. She was so nice. Cricket walked up and performed the gracious acceptance. Now it was Ashley and Tami. The girl next door versus the evil sexpot. Luke held the final rose. His face was serious, and then one corner of his mouth curved up.

"Ashley."

Yippee!! For a moment there she had doubted him and she didn't like the way it had felt. A grin covered her face as she walked up to accept the rose. Her eyes locked with his each step of the way. Euphoria ran through her. He liked her. He wanted her. It wasn't just a temporary thing.

"Will you accept this rose?" He held the rose close to his chest.

"Yes, I'll accept this rose." It felt like an out-of-body experience. As she put her fingers around the stem, he put his other hand around hers, holding it securely. Energy sizzled between them. Luke leaned down and kissed her lightly on the corner of her mouth. His cheek brushed against hers an extra moment. She walked away, floating on a cloud, and joined Cricket. They tipped their roses together in celebration.

Tami walked up to him, daggers in her eyes. "You jerk! You wouldn't know the perfect woman if she gave you a lap dance."

Luke roared with laughter.

Warmth and happiness filled Ashley. Luke glanced her way and winked.

Chapter Fourteen

Ashley peered out the small window of the private plane. The view was like nothing she'd seen before. Hills and valleys stretched as far as the eye could see. An endless forest covered the mountainous terrain. So, this was Louisiana. Ashley hadn't been this far south before, other than a trip to Orlando as a young teenager. This was a part of the U.S. she'd never known existed. It was much more vast than she'd imagined and majestic in the power of its natural beauty.

This was the place Luke, the superstar quarterback, called home.

So far she'd seen him polite and gracious. Most of the time cameras followed him around with a crowd of women at the mansion or on dates. Now he'd be on his own turf, surrounded by his people. Ashley wondered how he'd act. Would he be different? Would he be nervous about her meeting his family? She was.

There was quite a bit of turbulence on the flight. She hadn't eaten breakfast that morning, and the rumble of the plane matched her stomach. She felt nervous about meeting Luke's family and taking a step forward in their relationship.

Relationship. Was that what they had? It felt like a relationship, but the reality was that they were playing a foolish game in front of cameras. But Luke didn't make her feel foolish or nervous when they were together. He was getting under her skin and she liked it. He made her laugh a lot, and he was more complex than she would have guessed a big jock might be.

The thunk of the landing equipment lowering into place brought her back to the present. Off in the distance she saw a tiny airport. The small landing strip was close to Luke's hometown of Whiskey Bayou. Ashley tried to get a grip on her nerves and put on her game face. A couple of vehicles waited, with cameras in place. She felt blessed to have avoided a camera on the flight down. Apparently, without Luke, there was nothing to film. Speaking of being without Luke, she didn't see him, and there was no limo or town car waiting. Ashley wondered if she was to meet him at his parents' home. Yikes. She hoped not.

The plane landed smoothly and pulled up near the waiting crew. As the door opened, the pilot turned off the engines. Filled with a mixture of excitement and anxiety, Ashley stood on the top step of the portable stairs still looking for Luke. He was nowhere in sight. As she began to descend, the roar of a motorcycle in the distance stopped her.

She paused and watched the rider advance, dressed in faded jeans and black boots. He stopped near the base of the stairs, turned off the bike, and pulled off his helmet. Luke welcomed her with a smile and a wink.

"I thought you might like to enjoy the countryside in style." He motioned to the bike. A second helmet was hooked on the back.

Ashley dashed down the steps. Luke caught her in a huge hug, swinging her off her feet. He kissed her cheek and set her back down.

"I've missed you," he whispered, his arms around her waist, forehead pressed against hers.

"I've missed you too." She loved the feel of his arms around her.

Luke glanced at the producer. "Hey, Jim, can we go now?"

"Sure thing. Just don't drive too fast. We need to keep up."

Luke helped Ashley strap on the helmet, then showed her where to step to get on the motorcycle. The bike wasn't new by any means, but very nice, and far out of her price range.

Once Ashley settled in, Luke started the motor,

lifted the kickstand, and patted her on the leg. He said something, but she couldn't make it out over the noise of the cycle and the helmet on her head.

They took off and Ashley held on for dear life. Luke popped a wheelie down the runway. She tightened her hold around his waist, terrified. He must have told her to hold on tight.

When the front tire landed smoothly on the pavement, Luke accelerated. Ashley was part scared and part exhilarated. She'd only been on a motorcycle once before but hadn't been impressed. The big machines made her nervous. Too much power and too many chances to wipe out. But something about the way Luke controlled his motorcycle made her feel safe and protected.

He turned off at the end of the airstrip and headed for wide-open country roads. As they made the turn, Ashley saw the crew falling behind. It was obvious Luke wanted to lose their prying eyes, and she was elated. Time alone with him was a dream come true.

They cruised along the quiet roads and through wooded areas. She relaxed and eased her grip around his waist. He patted her hands as she settled in against his back. She smiled at their silent communication. They were unable to speak or look at each other, yet she felt connected to him, as though they could read each other's thoughts.

It felt good to lean against him, her arms wrapped snugly around him.

The warm breeze cooled them as they cruised swiftly. After twenty minutes he slowed and turned onto a side road. It wound around and up an incline. As Luke maneuvered the bike higher, he turned onto a narrow trail. It led through some brush and into a large clearing. He drove the bike up to the peak, parked and turned it off.

He pulled off his helmet and ran his lean fingers through his thick blond hair. He dismounted and turned to help Ashley as she fumbled with her strap. He released it easily and gently lifted off her helmet. Their eyes met. They were alone. He took her hand and helped her off the bike and into his arms. They held each other tightly, no words spoken.

It was impossible anyone could feel this good. What had she done to deserve this man? He was more than any woman could hope for.

Luke gazed down at her and kissed her waiting mouth. The caress of his lips set her aflame.

"I want to show you something." He took her hand and led her to a spot that overlooked the surrounding area. They could see for miles. Before them lay rolling hills thickly covered with trees. The terrain was like nothing she'd seen before. The clearing they stood in sloped to a small creek on one side of the property.

"It's beautiful," she said, gazing out over the landscape.

"It's mine," he stated with pride. "This is where I'm going to build my house. Right here, overlooking the hills." He took her hand and began to walk her around, pointing out where things would be built and how he planned to enjoy it. "Construction will start this summer. With any luck, by the end of the season, I can move in."

Ashley felt his excitement. He was creating his own home, a special place where he'd finally have his privacy and be able to enjoy the gifts of nature around him. And, even more special, Luke had shared this special place with her.

"It's going to be wonderful. I can't imagine how great it must feel to build your dream home, and in such a spectacular setting." She walked and picked wildflowers as she spoke. "I can see you here, sitting on the front porch, watching the sunset with a cold one in your hand." He smiled at her. "I can also see you whittling a piece of wood. Spitting tobacco juice and belching all night to keep the bugs away."

"Very funny."

"I love these," she said, picking another purple bloom.

"Those are weeds," he replied.

"They're not weeds. They're chicory, a wildflower."

"Whatever."

"Well, they're my favorite." She admired the small bouquet.

He led her back to his bike. "I suppose we should go find the film crew and start our date."

"Only if we have to."

"I don't want to get them too mad, plus I've got a lot to show you today. It's going to be great."

Ashley squeezed his hand. Yes, it was definitely going to be a great day.

"Incoming!" Luke's younger brother Mike shouted, tossing another crayfish into the pontoon boat. It landed with a thunk and quickly attempted a getaway, scuttling along the floor.

"Eek!" Ashley couldn't help screaming each time another of the shellfish landed. The ugly little critters were about four inches in length with black beady eyes and long tentacles. Luke snatched up a few and tossed them in a bucket, splashing out more water each time.

"Heads up," Mike called as another crawfish flew by her head.

Mike was a couple of inches shorter than Luke with a much stockier build. Ashley soon discovered he was a rascal with quick wit and a winning smile. He was also a shameless flirt.

"These'll be great before dinner," Luke said, tossing another into the bucket as Mike climbed back aboard.

"You're going to eat them?" Ashley crinkled her face in disgust. She was famished, but wasn't about to eat the gross crustaceans.

"No. *We* are going to eat them," Mike said, putting his wet arms around Ashley and pulling her close.

"That's right. Mom will be thrilled. We'll boil them

as soon as we get back." Luke leaned over the bucket to count how many they'd caught.

Suddenly, Ashley felt a sharp pinch in her backside. "Ouch." She turned to see Mike with a suggestive grin and raised eyebrows.

"What's wrong?" Luke looked up from counting the creepy fish.

"Nothing—something just bit me." She stepped closer to Luke, out of Mike's reach.

"Let's get these babies cooked. You can have the first one," Luke offered.

"No, thanks," she said from the safety of his side. "I wouldn't know how to eat it anyway."

"I'll teach you," offered Mike. "You just bite 'em, suck 'em, and shuck 'em. Right Luke?" Mike imitated the motions, staring at her as he went. "Rascal" did not do him justice, after all.

"So, Ashley, are you enjoying your visit?" Gus, Luke's dad, asked. It was obvious where Luke's size came from. Gus was tall, carrying the extra bulk that middle age invites. He sat at the head of the table, his presence dominating the room.

"Yes, thank you. It's been quite an adventure." Ashley smiled. "I had no idea such an amazing place existed. I've never traveled to this part of the country before. It is such a beautiful and wild place. You must love it here."

"Well, thank you, we do. In fact, the Townsends

have been in this area for more than two hundred and fifty years. We have a rich tradition of family here. We hold it near and dear. Right, Luke?" He gestured to Luke with his fork. "Our boy here is like a diamond in the rough. He came out of this wild place and grew into something real special."

Ashley smiled and nodded as she listened to Luke's dad. Luke was indeed a diamond. The kind of rare and special person you didn't meet often. "You would have to look long and hard to find another person like him anywhere, I'm sure."

For the first time in her life, she put a spoonful of black-eyed peas in her mouth.

"Speaking of looking, sweetie," said Maxine, Luke's mom. "How long have you been looking to hitch up with a nice boy like our Luke?"

"Excuse me?" Ashley choked. She wasn't sure if it was the peas or the question. "I wouldn't exactly say I have been looking to 'hitch up' with anyone."

"No?" asked Gus. "Well then, what exactly are you doing if you're not trying to find a man?"

Ashley glanced at Luke for a hint as to how to answer the question. He shrugged.

She hesitated while swallowing the vile peas, unsure how to proceed. "Well, I came here to spend more time with Luke. I've had such a wonderful time getting to know him and he kindly invited me to meet all of you. Today has been a special treat."

They all looked at her. Was there food in her teeth?

Did she imagine the oppressive silence, or was it real? Luke didn't seem to notice as he shoveled a mystery vegetable in his mouth. It must be okra, or squash, or some other scary food Ashley'd never encountered.

"Then why did you enter this contest?" asked Mike. "Isn't this set up so you all compete to marry the rich dude?"

How could she possibly answer his question truthfully? Yes, it was a contest to find a husband. Yes, it was a competition, but she hadn't entered it on purpose, and she didn't want to get married. Not now and not for a long time. What could she say? The evil cameras rolled quietly in the corner, catching every word. What should she say? Ashley took a deep breath and hoped whatever sputtered out of her mouth sounded honest and heartfelt.

"Yes, I did enter this contest," she lied. "And for many the goal is to marry the—how did you say it?— rich dude." Ashley nodded toward his now-quietly-observing brother. "However, I'd like to believe I'm different than the other women."

Mike rolled his eyes.

"I was looking for a little adventure and a change of pace in life, and I must certainly say this has been it. Wouldn't you agree, Luke?" She smiled over at him.

"Can't argue with that," Luke agreed. "We have certainly enjoyed our adventures, and life with you is definitely a change of pace." He eyed her mischievously.

Was that a compliment or not? she wondered.

"So, what do you do for a living, Ashley?" asked Luke's mother.

Slightly embarrassed, she admitted, "Right now, I'm doing this quirky reality show on competing to marry a bachelor."

His brother nodded pointedly at his father.

She tried to bring some levity to the conversation and quickly added, "I am actually between jobs at the moment and using this opportunity to try something fun and different."

"So, you've been leading him on throughout this whole little game show? Is that what you're saying?" Gus questioned. "You're playing with my son's emotions."

"Oh my gosh, no! I would never lead anyone on. Luke and I have shared some great times together, and I think we have a lot in common."

Luke snorted with laughter. She looked at him in disbelief. What was so funny?

"Don't you think you're exaggerating a bit? You don't golf, you don't hunt, you don't like sports, and you're afraid of wildlife. Ashley, I know we have a couple things in common, but a *lot*?"

Who was this man, and was he really the same guy she'd shown up with? Or was his family somehow changing him? She was more confused than ever. "It was my impression that we both enjoyed humor and interesting conversation."

"Yes, and that's about it." Luke gave her a broad wink.

Before she could respond, Mike entered the fray. "Luke's always been successful with the ladies. Even the ugly ones. I have to admit, the way you looked at me earlier today made me wonder if I was finally going to beat my brother at something." Mike winked at her. What was with the men in this family and the winking?

Mike continued. "If Luke doesn't pick you, maybe you'll settle for me."

Her jaw dropped. She looked to Luke for his support. This was getting out of hand. Luke gave Mike a cold stare.

"Don't feel bad," said Luke's mother. "We get this all the time with Luke. He's such a ladies' man. No one can resist him. You don't have to feel bad about playing your best hand for him. We understand. We're used to it."

His father interrupted. "You know you'd have to sign a pre-nup if you win this contest? You don't just get all his money."

"I don't want his money!" Ashley was stunned. Why would he say that? What a terrible man. How could Luke tolerate their behavior?

"Well then, what is it you do want with him?"

"Nothing. Absolutely nothing." She couldn't sit there and be attacked any longer. She stood, her stomach churning, and looked at Maxine. "Thank you for welcoming me to your home." Then she looked at the rest of the group and added, "And thank you for all of the hospitality extended to me." Ashley stepped away from the table and pushed in her chair. "Enjoy your dinner."

She grabbed her purse from the table in the hall and walked out the front door.

She didn't look back.

"What in the world were you doing?" Luke shouted in disbelief.

"You said we could tease her, that she had a sense of humor," said Mike.

"I said you could tease her—not rake her over the coals."

His family all sat quietly, looking guilty.

"I'm sorry, honey. We didn't mean to hurt her," said his mom. "She seems like a very nice girl. You should know, the producer, Jim, told us to put her on the spot. He said it would make a better show. Otherwise he said it would be boring."

"Well, it sure wasn't boring, was it? Do you realize you looked like a bunch of uneducated hicks? White trash."

"We did, didn't we? Susan is going to kill me when she hears about this," Mike said, referring to his wife.

"Now I understand why she refused to be a part of this. She knew what you had planned." Luke glared at Mike.

"You'd better go after her," said his mother. "She'll be halfway to Mississippi by now."

Luke shoved his chair out of the way. "I'll deal with you later," he said pointedly to Mike.

"What? What'd I do?"

"Mike, shut up." Gus cuffed him upside the head.

Luke stormed out of the house.

Ashley walked hastily down the long drive, away from the Townsend home.

"Ashley, wait," Luke's voice called.

Her pace picked up as she reached the road.

Luke caught up and took her by the shoulder. "Please don't leave."

"Don't," she said, pulling away from him, her blood still boiling from their insults.

"They didn't mean anything," Luke said, his face full of concern.

"Didn't mean anything?" she shouted, infuriated. "Open your eyes, Luke! They hated me and wanted to make sure both you and I knew it!"

"No, they were playing around. They do it to everyone." He took her hand and tried to soothe her. "Don't worry, they like you just fine."

"Oh sure, Mike loved me! He kept pinching my butt and winking at me every time you turned your back." Her temper was rising. "I thought I was going to scream! Or slug him. That's what I should have done!"

"Ignore Mike. He can be a jerk sometimes."

"No! I'm not going to ignore it! I have more respect

for myself than that. He's a creep! I'm sorry. I know he's your brother and you love him, but he is."

She turned onto the main gravel road. It was worn, with more chicory growing on the shoulder.

"Come on, Ashley, calm down. Don't you think you're overreacting a bit?"

"Overreacting!" She turned back, waving her hands in the air. "You think this is overreacting? You ain't seen nothing yet!" She pointed a finger in his face. "Don't push me, Luke. I'm in no mood." She continued stomping toward town, her face pinched in anger.

"Ashley, wait, we have to talk."

"You want to talk? Fine! Let's freaking talk." She came back at him, fists on hips. "Your father thinks I'm playing with your emotions and that I'm a gold digger, your brother thinks I'm free for the taking, and your mother thinks I'm a bimbo. I'm surprised the dog didn't bite me!"

"Ashley, they didn't mean anything, and you're taking this way too seriously. Calm down."

"Taking this too seriously?" she asked in disbelief. "You sat there and let them attack me. What was that about? Listen, Luke, when someone attacks me, I bleed, okay? And when I get cornered, I fight back. Your family cornered me and it took everything in me just to be respectful and walk away, which is a lot more than I can say for them—or for you." She turned back, fuming as she marched down the road, then paused and came back.

"Oh, and thanks so much for the big vote of confidence. I really felt your support back there. Especially with your line, 'A lot in common? Don't you think you're exaggerating a bit'?"

"You don't understand," Luke said.

"No, *you* don't understand," she said, beginning to yell in earnest. The cameraman followed her every move. "You understand nothing! Nothing at all! I didn't want to embarrass myself on this show. You knew it better than anyone and what did you do? You sat by while I turned into a crazed lunatic," she yelled, shaking her hands in the air. "You let your family tear me apart in front of the cameras. I've lost it. I've fallen over the edge of sanity."

Luke stood frozen in place, his eyes wide.

"Look at me, Luke! I'm on national television and the world is going to know I'm a freaking loser!" she screamed. "I'll never be able to show my face again. I'll be known as the crazy gold-digging loser from 'Love 'Em or Leave 'Em.'" She couldn't stop herself. She wanted to, but all her pent-up emotions and tension from the last few weeks had sprung. Everything was coming out and she couldn't stop it. "I guess this is where you leave 'em, huh?"

Luke winced.

Ashley's tone changed. "Wow, the ratings are *really* going to go sky-high with my performance." She mocked a smile. "Whew! Bet you're proud to be on a winning football team *and* a hit TV show! You sure are great! And some lucky chick is gonna get you! Oops, be sure to tell her about the pre-nup before your dad does. You don't want to shock a gal again. Who knows how she'll react?"

"Ashley, please," Luke tried again, his voice soft to calm her hysteria. She was over-the-top and the cameraman continued to follow. It was all on film and there wasn't a thing he could do about it.

"Ashley." He stood in front of her, blocking the camera, his hands on her shoulders.

"Calm down? Right!" Tears ran freely, her hair stuck out, and her eyes darted about wildly. "Do me a favor, okay?" She cried openly. He watched, not knowing how to help. "Can't you do just one thing for me?"

"Sure," he answered, his voice filled with compassion. "Anything. What can I do?"

"At the next rose ceremony, don't you dare give me a rose." She sobbed. "I don't care if I never see another rose for the rest of my life."

His heart was breaking. All he wanted to do was ease her pain. But he didn't want to lose her, either. He stood silently, full of indecision.

"What? You can't even manage that?"

"Okay." His voice were soft and barely audible. "Not another rose."

"Didn't anyone ever tell you? Roses stink!"

She started back down the road and hailed down an old pickup truck rumbling toward them. It was old man Walker on his daily trip to town. She asked for a ride and hopped in the cab before he could answer. Walker looked at Luke questioningly, and he nodded for them to go ahead. Old Walk would be kind to her and make sure she arrived safely. She couldn't be in better hands. Ashley put sunglasses on over her blotchy face and never looked back.

Luke watched the ancient truck drive away until it was out of sight. With a sigh, he turned toward home, his head hung low, the infernal cameraman still following. What had happened? How had things gone from so great to so bad, without him realizing it until it was too late? He didn't blame Ashley, though. His family had insulted her character and attacked her pride. All of it in front of those blasted cameras. Ashley was right. The show would love this and she would look like a fool. There was nothing he could do about it. Plus, he needed to bring Cricket to meet his parents in two days. What a mess.

And this show was supposed to be fun.

Ashley caught a bus north out of Podunk, Louisiana, and cried all the way to Tennessee. After changing buses, she slept most of the way back to Wisconsin.

She never did eat that day.

"Why are you in Madison? I hear you practically shut down production. What is going on?"

"I quit, Kel. It's over." Ashley's voice was flat and void of emotion.

"What do you mean 'it's over'? Talk to me. Spill it."

"No, I'm not going to spill it," she said. "Suffice it to say, any shred of dignity I had left is now gone." Not to mention the shape her heart was in, which was in shreds. She'd fallen hard and fast. She made Rachel and Gwen look like naïve beginners when it came to falling hard. She had bared her soul. Now it felt as though she'd been trampled by the entire Packer team. No bandage could heal her wound. Maybe time would numb the pain, but the humiliation would take much longer. With the whole fiasco about to hit the TV waves, there'd be nowhere to hide, and she hadn't even finished the show.

"I'm sure it's not as bad as you think. You're just emotional right now."

"Go watch the dailies, Kelli. It's all there in Technicolor," she said, wallowing in self-pity. "I know what I did and what I said. And those bosses of yours are going to show every frame of it."

"It's okay," her friend responded.

Silence. Then, "I'm not going back," she said.

"I'm sorry, Ashley, but you have to."

"No, Kelli, I don't." For once she wasn't going to budge. "It's about time I stood up for myself, and it starts now. I've spent too much time being taken advantage of and played for a fool. I won't let it happen again." Ashley paced back and forth in the small space of her kitchen, one arm held protectively across her middle. "You know I love you and would do anything for you, but this has gone beyond the bounds of friendship. I never signed a contract. Beyond my loyalty to you, I don't owe anything to anyone. I need you to do something for me. I want the scene pulled off the air." She prayed it would happen.

"Listen, I wish I could let you walk away from this, but I can't. You're a pivotal part of the show. You're in the top two. You're unconventional. The producers say the audience is going to love you. You'll be the media darling."

"I'm nobody's media darling, and you know it. I can't stand those stupid cameras and I'm not doing any media." She paused and took a breath for strength. "I made a total fool of myself at Luke's—it was awful. I stood there ranting and raving and blubbering while the dim-witted camera guy recorded my every move." The memory of the experience rushed back, causing her stomach to roll.

"I'm sure it's not so bad."

"It's bad. Kelli, I did the ugly cry." She cringed, as she recalled the experience.

"You didn't!"

"Oh yeah, I did. This tops it all. I am now in the 'pull a fit' Hall of Fame."

"I'm so sorry, hon. I really am, but please, Ashley, you can't quit." There was sincere desperation in her voice. "If you leave, we're left with nothing. You've become an anchor of the show." She hesitated. "I need you to come back."

Ashley's internal battle intensified. Everything in her gut screamed "Don't go!" It hurt so bad, how could she possibly put herself through more humiliation? Besides, seeing Luke again was more than she could bear.

"Kel, I don't know if I can. I understand how important this is to your career, and I would never want to ruin this for you, but I have nothing left to give. I have no idea how to recover enough to face it again."

"It will be okay." Kelli sounded hopeful. "I'll take care of everything and I will be there for you. It'll be made clear to the producers not to push. There's only a few days left and I'll make it as smooth as possible." She paused and remained quiet for a moment, then added. "He wants you back."

"What?"

"Luke. He wants you back."

"No way! I can't. Oh, Kelli. Why'd you bring him up?"

"One, because he's the star of the show. And two, because he likes you."

"I highly doubt it after the way I behaved."

"He feels terrible. The producers had told his family to make it interesting."

"It was interesting, all right."

"Here's the deal. The show is almost over. There are only three days between now and the final ceremony. You and Cricket have one more date each and then the entire thing is done."

Tears welled in her eyes as she battled against herself. "Fine. I won't quit, but please don't push me right now. I can't take it." Her voice quivered. She felt fragile, like a crystal vase riding on a rumbling train to destruction. "Just help me survive until the end of this show and never ask me for another favor the rest of my life."

"All right," Kelli said. "I know this turned into so much more than either of us thought it would, and I'm sorry for all the embarrassment you've gone through, but come on, Ashley. You must like him too, don't you? You've spent a lot of time together."

That was the biggest part of the problem. She did like him. Too much. She hated feeling vulnerable. She'd wanted to make a good impression on his family, but it had all fallen apart. And they had attacked her. They'd made her look like a fool. She still burned from the experience.

How could he possibly want her after her Dr. Jekyll and Mr. Hyde performance?

"I don't like him enough to ruin my life any longer."

"Please. Just three more days. I'll have a ticket waiting for you at the airport. The time will zip by."

"Only if my conditions are agreed upon up front."

"Fine. What do you need? A bigger trailer?"

"Smart aleck. No, I want the scene cut!"

"But Ashley, it's great TV."

"Geez, Kelli, take your career hat off for just a minute and put your best-friend hat on. I don't care what it is. I don't want the world to see it."

"All right. I'll talk to the editor. But I really need you to come through for me and get yourself back here."

"One more thing. I want to keep as much distance from Luke as possible. No more parties or get-to-know-you games. I'll go on one final date, but it has to be plain and simple. No overnights, no families, no surprises. Short and sweet."

"I don't think any of it will be a problem."

"Good. And when this thing is over, I want to be left alone. I am not doing any interviews, posing for pictures, or after-show whatevers. I'm done." She remembered Luke mentioning all the promotions done with shows like these. She wasn't taking any chances. "Kelli, if they won't agree, I'm not coming back. I got on this show at the last minute, and I never signed a contract. I don't want any offers of money. I just want to be left alone. Got it?"

"Okay, I'll do everything I can. Now get some rest. I'll call you back when I have your flight booked." She hesitated, then added, "Ash, I never thought it would turn out this way."

"I know."

"And Ashley?"

"Yeah."

"I'm so sorry."

"Me too."

Chapter Fifteen

L ife hadn't changed much at the mansion, other than the number of people in it. Cricket was on her meet-the-parents visit with Luke, which didn't elicit one iota of jealousy from Ashley. Her first instinct upon returning had been to hide in her room the entire time. Then she thought, who cares? If the cameramen wanted to follow her around the house and tape her every move, fine. She had nothing left to hide.

She found a corner near the pool where the trees reached over her, creating a dappled blanket of leaves and flowers that allowed just enough sunlight in to keep her wrapped in a cocoon of warm air and fresh scents. From where she sat, Ashley enjoyed a perfect view of the lush landscape enclosing the pool area. It was a small piece of heaven in an otherwise turbulent world.

Ashley read trashy novels to keep her mind off her train wreck of a life. She drank a never-ending supply of Diet Pepsi and munched on crackers and fruit. Mostly she napped, safe in her little haven. She felt depleted, empty, and would need a whole lot of energy to face the next couple of days. She knew of no other way to prepare for what was to come.

If the camera guy was prepared to film "Stupid Midwestern Girl Entertains World Again," he must be bored to tears by now. The network could have saved their money and let him go home. She would not embarrass herself again.

On the afternoon of the second day, Cricket returned from meeting Luke's family. Ashley's taut nerves were ready to snap at any moment.

"Are you okay, Ashley? Something seems wrong."

"No, I'm fine. Everything's fine," Ashley said, masking her emotions.

"Are you sure? You seem upset. Did something happen?"

"Nope, nothing happened." Her eyes welled up with tears. "Nothing's wrong."

Cricket nodded compassionately. "All right, whatever you say."

"That's what I say," Ashley replied stoically.

"Okay." Cricket walked over and hugged her gently.

Ashley tapped the stem of her margarita glass repeatedly with her fingernail, avoiding Luke's eyes as they faced each other over tortilla chips and salsa at a rustic little restaurant named Paco's. Luke's beer sat untouched and angst etched his face. Small red recording lights dotted the room, reminding Ashley of the cameras' ever-present intrusion. A three-piece band prepared to play in the corner.

"Ashley."

She stopped tapping.

"Please let me explain what happened with my family."

"No." She slapped her hand with finality on the table, her voice filled with warning.

"We've got to talk."

"No, we don't." She glanced at one of the cameras and spoke quietly. "Not like this."

Understanding lit his eyes. "Okay." He leaned back in his chair as the band began to play. The catchy music lightened the mood in the room. Ashley sipped her ice water and felt relieved that Luke wasn't pushing her. Her fingers kept time to the music. Luke's eyes lit up. He placed his hand over hers. Her hand froze.

"Dance with me," he said, a smile lifting the corners of his mouth.

Ashley hesitated. The music was loud. The sound equipment and cameras would have trouble following them. "Sure." Besides, it was better than avoiding each other all evening.

Luke squeezed her hand and led her onto the dance floor. The band began a new number, "Mambo No. 5."

He twirled her around dramatically, then quickly pulled her into his arms.

"Smooth moves," she commented.

He led her through some swing steps she'd never done before. It took a few steps to catch on, but Luke was a strong lead and guided her easily through twirls, behind-the-back exchanges, and turns.

The feel of his hands on her waist guiding her around the dance floor made her feel protected and alive. She relaxed as she forgot about the cameras and all the traumas of the last week and laughed playfully with Luke through three fast-paced songs.

When the band changed to a slow song, Luke twirled her into his arms, pulled her close, and molded her to his body. Ashley put her arms around his neck and leaned into him, her forehead pressed to his cheek. Her heart pounded next to his chest—she wasn't sure if her pounding pulse was from the dancing or from her nearness to Luke. His firm body felt warm against her, the scent of his aftershave a reminder of their times together.

He gazed at her.

She smiled and tilted her face up. "Where did a guy like you learn to dance like this?"

"What do you mean 'a guy like me'?" he asked, raising an eyebrow.

"You know what I mean. How does a tough jock learn all those smooth moves?"

"Arthur Murray, baby," he said, swinging her around.

"No way. I cannot see you in dance lessons."

"You're right. Growing up, the town always held big festivals every summer. One of the highlights was the dances each night. Everyone would be there and dance all night. It was a great way for us teenage boys to get close to the girls!"

"Why am I not surprised?" She shook her head.

Luke suddenly spun them around. Ashley held on tightly. What was it about this man? He made her feel so good, even after all the drama. She relaxed into his hold.

Luke leaned his mouth near her ear and whispered, "I'm sorry about the bayou."

She pulled away briefly. "I don't want to talk about it, please?"

After a moment, he nodded, kissed her on the forehead and pulled her close once again. They danced two slow songs, with Luke nuzzling her neck, whispering in her ear and making her laugh.

Click. Click. Click. Luke leaned back against the bed's headboard flipping through the TV channels, checking scores.

He was dressed. But not ready. He'd showered and shaved. His hair held the perfect amount of gel and he smelled of his favorite aftershave. But he wasn't ready.

TV didn't help either. He pulled his cell phone from his shirt pocket and hit Redial. It rang several times.

"Yeah?"

"Hey, Mike."

"Is it over yet?"

"Hasn't started."

"Bummer."

"That's an understatement." Luke clicked the remote again.

"So, who are you going to pick?"

"Heck if I know."

"No kidding."

Silence filled the phone line.

"Mike, remember when you had to pick between the job you wanted in Atlanta or Susan? How did you make the decision?"

"Aw, I don't know."

"Come on, Mike, I need some help here."

"Follow your gut. Sometimes in life it's not about what you want, but what you can't live without. You might not know if something is best for you, but you do know you'll always regret it if you don't find out."

"Huh," Luke grunted.

"Okay, I met both of them, but I want you to describe them."

"Well, Cricket is smart and sweet. She's a great golfer, likes sports, and has a nice family. She comes from money, so she understands what comes with it. She even wants to teach kids. She's perfect."

"So pick her."

"But then there's Ashley." He couldn't quite wrap his thoughts around his feelings for her. "Ashley has a smart mouth, and she makes me laugh. She doesn't like sports, but she has a heart of gold. Her family is dysfunctional, and she's not comfortable with a lot of outside attention." He wondered if she could adjust to his life in the spotlight. "I can't figure her out."

"This doesn't need to be so hard, Luke. Who makes you happy? Who could you see yourself waking up to every day? That's the one you should pick."

"Hmm," Luke grumbled.

"And if you still can't decide, then just pick the one that kisses better."

"You're a lot of help. Thanks for nothing." Luke flipped the phone shut and tossed it on the bed. He stood and walked over to the mirror. He wrapped his tie around his neck, folding and flipping it as he went. He slid the knot up to his neck, and it felt like a noose tightening.

Chapter Sixteen

F resh flowers transformed the pool area into a breath-taking garden, complete with shrubs and trees covered with twinkle lights providing a sprinkle of soft light. Flowering azaleas and hydrangeas made a pathway to a small gazebo where pink roses climbed up the sides. The air held a delicate sweet scent. Waves crashed against the shore in the distance. The sound echoed the feeling in Ashley's heart. On the outside she looked beautiful and tranquil, but on the inside her heart crashed against her chest in fear and anticipation of the ceremony ahead.

Common sense told her the nightmare would soon be over and she could escape this insanity. But deep inside she didn't want her time with Luke to end. He was special and she didn't want to lose whatever it was they had.

She needed to gear up for this final scene. Afterward she could get her life back in order, away from the prying eye of the cameras.

The door to her bedroom opened and Kelli walked in. "You okay?" she asked tentatively.

"I'm fine." Ashley took a deep breath and tried to remain calm.

"You sure, honey?" Kelli sat next to her on the bed and took Ashley's hand in hers. "Honestly, I never expected in a million years that you and I would be sitting here tonight for the finale."

"Me neither." She took another deep breath for courage. "So, what's the plan here? How much longer do I have to be tortured before I get to drive off into the sunset?"

"Not long now." Kelli looked at her watch and switched into business mode. "The rose ceremony set is in place and all cameras and lights are ready for action. We're prepared to start whenever you are."

A chill of fear quickly ran through Ashley. She saw the concern wash over Kelli's face.

"It'll be over soon. Hang in there." Kelli stood and walked to the door. "I hope it turns out the way you want." She opened the door and looked back one last time. "Come down as soon as you're ready. And Ashley, thanks. You know how much it means to me." The door closed quietly behind her.

Kelli's words echoed in her head. "I hope it turns out the way you want."

Ashley only wished she knew how she wanted things to turn out. As much as she hoped the torture of this insane show to be over with, her gut told her that what she and Luke had was very real and not something found often.

But there was no way she would accept a rose from him. He'd humiliated her and brought out her worst side in front of the cameras. She didn't want to be hounded by the press over their relationship on the show. He would pick Cricket. She was great and was a much better match for Luke.

After another deep breath, Ashley stood, ready to face the cameras. She took one final glance in the mirror; even she had to admit she looked amazing. Her hard-earned tan made her skin glow. The copper-colored dress clung to her figure in all the right places. Thin straps lay gently on her shoulders as the dress gracefully came together in a deep vee, showing off a bit of cleavage.

Not bad, she thought to herself. *At least I'll go out looking good.*

Downstairs, the producers and crew waited. After quickly reviewing where to walk and stand, the final filming began. She stood just outside the doors of the mansion for the last time and overlooked the beautiful spectacle created in the pool area. Ashley took a deep breath for courage and nodded her okay to begin.

The cameras rolled.

"Ashley, Luke is standing in the gazebo waiting for you. This is the moment you have been waiting for," Clay said in his TV voice. "This is when you find out if Luke has a rose and a proposal for you, or if he is saying good-bye forever." Clay stepped aside and gestured with his hand for her to make her way along the path to her destiny.

Each step brought Ashley closer to the answer and the end. She felt more confidence as she moved toward Luke. Whatever happened, she would not embarrass herself. It would all be over in a matter of minutes. She'd learned the hard way that there were no second takes in reality TV.

As she walked around the curve of ficus trees, she saw the gazebo. In the center Luke waited. He looked incredible. He gave off an aura of self-assurance, standing there in a cream-colored shirt and dark slacks. The colors enhanced his great looks and blond hair. Subdued lighting created a romantic ambience. Next to him, on a white pillar, a single red rose waited.

Luke looked up and gave Ashley a warm and rather weary smile. She could tell that this wasn't a walk in the park for him either.

"Hey there," Luke reached out his hand to help her up the steps to the gazebo.

Ashley looked into his eyes. There was a serious set to them. What did it mean?

And then she tripped.

Luke's other hand shot out and quickly steadied her so she didn't end up on the floor before him.

Unbelievable! She'd done it again! She'd been so busy looking into Luke's eyes that she hadn't thought about lifting her dress to climb the steps. She should be humiliated, but instead she started to laugh.

"Your reflexes are getting better."

"I've been practicing in my downtime. Looks like it came in handy." He held her elbow as he gazed into her eyes.

"I guess we'd better get started," Luke said, "before the natives get restless."

"Ready when you are," she lied.

Suddenly the air seemed a little too still and a bit too warm. The feel of cameras filming from every angle made her claustrophobic. Luke took both her hands in his and gave them a small squeeze for reassurance, as though he could read her thoughts and see the dread she felt at this finale.

"This has been quite an adventure," he began with a sigh. "When I agreed to be part of this show, I wasn't sure what to expect. I really did hope I could find someone who would be a match for me, but I didn't believe it could actually happen."

Ashley couldn't begin to guess what direction he was going with this.

"I have spent the past ten years in and out of the media spotlight. Sometimes it was at the highest points in

my life, and sometimes the lowest. While it can be dis-
ruptive to my life, I've come to respect the people
whose job it is to do the reporting, take the photos, or
catch it all on film. Don't get me wrong—there are
times it makes me crazy. But it's their job, as much as
playing football is mine.

"I say all of this because I also understand that this
has not been a part of your life. You came here not realizing the full impact of cameras recording your every
move, whether it was hitting a great hole of golf, or
falling on your face in front of millions." He squeezed
her hands again and the corner of his mouth turned up
in a smile.

"Ashley, you have captured my heart . . ." She
looked at him with loving appreciation. "You have
captured my heart and kept me guessing and smiling
all the time." He leaned back and held her at arm's
length again, giving her one of his trademark devilish
looks.

Everything flew through her mind at once. What was
he thinking? Did he want her as badly as she wanted
him? Was he willing to pick her after she'd lost her cool
at his family's home? Her heart was in her hand and he
was holding it. Could she turn down the rose if he gave
it to her? Did she want to?

"Thank you for making this crazy ride such a pleasure. You are a shining star. You are gutsy. You never
hesitate to speak your mind or let me know where I
stand. In the circles I move in, those qualities are rare.

You are genuine, and you'll never know how much you mean to me."

He paused and licked his lips as though trying to make a difficult decision. He took a deep breath and gave her a nervous smile. It filled her heart to over-flowing. He truly cared about her and it made her glow.

"As I said before, in the beginning I was skeptical, yet hopeful of finding someone special who might change my life. Ashley, you have always been a joy to be with, and I have been thoughtless and blasé about your feelings."

Ashley shook her head in denial.

"No, I have—it's true. You've given me everything and never asked for anything back. In return, I have embarrassed you and pushed you to your breaking point and beyond.

"It was unforgivable, but now I know what you're made of."

Ashley looked up at him, confused at his confession.

"And it's some pretty strong stuff. But"—he hesitated—"even steel will break under enough pressure. I asked my family to tease you a bit to see how you would react. Then the producers asked them to badger you with questions. I had no idea they would take it so far, and for that I'm truly sorry. So are they."

Ashley couldn't believe it. He'd asked them to treat her that way. He'd set her up and she'd lost it. They must think her an absolute fool.

* * *

Being near her was painful. She was perfect. Ashley's sun-kissed skin and honey-blond hair moved gently in the light breeze. Everything about her fit an imaginary ideal he didn't realize he'd created.

Luke struggled. What he wanted to do and what he felt he must do were two different things. Would she forgive him regardless of which direction he went? He just didn't know. She looked at him with such hesitation. He was afraid that, whatever he did, she would again feel embarrassed on national TV. The show hadn't even aired, but he knew the fallout would be huge. She was so lovable. He was sure the viewing audiences would want to follow her every move and know everything about her. It complicated his decision even more.

"We have come to the end of the journey. Thank you for this amazing ride . . . And now—" He paused, and looked deeply into her eyes. His voice grew husky. "I let you go. You are free from this crazy circus."

Ashley froze, gazing up at him. Her hands were still tightly embraced in his. He was sending her away.

There was no rose for her.

No future for them.

This was what she had wanted, wasn't it? She'd demanded more than once that he not give her more roses. He'd promised and now he stood by it. Or perhaps his heart had never belonged to her at all.

Luke watched her, unspoken words in his eyes. He

seemed concerned about her reaction. Shoot, she didn't know how she felt. Devastated? Relieved?

She pulled herself together and looked at him, her eyes glistening.

She leaned up and whispered in his ear, her cheek brushing gently against his, "Thank you."

Ashley gave his hands one final squeeze, then released them and the loving hold they had on her. She turned and slowly retraced her steps down the floral path and away from Luke.

It was over.

Her wish had finally come true. She was off the show. She could start fresh and put it all out of her mind.

Except for the fact that it meant Luke would be choosing Cricket. With that, the bottom of her world fell away.

The rest of the night passed in a blur. Ashley went through the motions in stunned silence as she was directed toward the waiting limo to whisk her away from paradise and back to the bleak world of true reality, not something manufactured by Hollywood.

At one point, she saw Kelli try to catch her eye, but she didn't feel up to being fawned over or pitied by her friend. She needed to get away. They put her into the limo along with one of the producers and a cameraman hoping to catch her sobbing confessions of how she'd fallen deeply in love and couldn't believe he would go on without her.

Mostly, she felt shock and tremendous loss. She loved him and he was gone.

The producer peppered her with questions. How did she feel? Was she surprised? What would she do next?

Looking into the camera, she struggled to appear happy with the outcome she'd asked for. "It was a wonderful opportunity for me to be on this show and get to know so many terrific people," she said methodically, struggling to control her emotions. "I know everything turned out exactly as it should have. I wish Luke and Cricket the absolute best. They will make a wonderful couple."

Ashley refused to make another statement or answer any other questions. She'd given far more of herself than she'd ever intended. Let the producers be angry. She was done. It was over.

Two hours later, the show wrapped. The outcome was not what the producers had expected, but it certainly would get a lot of attention.

Luke took a final look around at the now-empty pool area, recalling all the memories of the past two months. The lights were turned off and the camera crew had departed.

He looked down and saw the single rose lying on the pillar. He picked it up, brought it to his nose and inhaled deeply. He broke it in half and tossed it to the ground. "She was right. Roses really do stink."

Chapter Seventeen

One month later

Ashley walked into her apartment and tossed her keys onto the sideboard next to the front door while juggling mail, purse, and shopping bags. She hit Play on the answering machine as she passed into the kitchen. Kelli's voice came on the machine. Her friend wouldn't give up. She felt responsible for the pain and sadness she had caused Ashley. Granted, Ashley never would have been on the show if it weren't for Kelli, but she wasn't angry and didn't blame Kelli for any of it. Sometimes life is hard and you have to deal with it. Kelli, however, wouldn't accept it. She'd made it her mission to pull Ashley out of her slump. Ashley loved her dearly, but needed space to heal and time to put her life back together.

221

Unfortunately, she kept hoping for a call from Luke. He'd never said he would call and she had never asked him to. But their parting had been so much less than ideal. She wanted a chance for closure, and to express her gratitude for all the kind things he'd said at the rose ceremony when he had taken the blame for all the craziness. But she had never gotten the chance to let him know how much his kindness meant. She'd fallen hard for him, but had let her stubborn pride keep her from giving them a chance. Now she was alone and Luke was with Cricket. She fought to keep her emotions at a distance. She had become numb to protect herself.

Ashley deleted Kelli's message. She'd call when she was ready to rehash it all, but now she needed to focus on her future. She'd started a new job. It was a great opportunity and she wanted to consume herself with work for a while. Promos for the show had already begun to air and the broadcast would begin in another week. She wanted to keep her nose to the grindstone so no one would notice her connection to the show. If she was lucky, the most she'd be was a blip on the local radar . . . she hoped.

Three months later

"Ashley, you need to see this," Kelli insisted for the umpteenth time.

"No, I don't," Ashley replied stubbornly from Kelli's hotel kitchenette. "I lived it and that was more than I could handle. I'm trying to move forward, not backward, here."

The last few weeks had become increasingly difficult. "Love 'Em or Leave 'Em" grew more popular with every episode. Ashley's recognition grew each day as she stopped for gas or went to the store, let alone actually tried to go out socially. The producers insisted she not date until after the final show aired. Not too hard to argue with that.

She still felt the pain even though many weeks had passed since the final taping. Most of the time she was able to hide it from herself and pretend life was fine. However, she mourned losing Luke. He was the most amazing person she'd ever met. When she had been with Luke, she'd felt whole, as if something had been missing before she'd met him. It was stupid and trite and probably no more than schoolgirl infatuation. Face it, the situation was anything but normal. So, why couldn't she get him out of her mind and out of her heart?

Kelli had hounded her for two weeks to get together to watch the final episode. All Ashley wanted to do was stay home, like the hermit she'd become, and eat chocolate chips with peanut butter. Finally, she'd given in when Kelli had said it would help her put closure to the situation. Closure was a good thing and she needed to move on. She didn't look forward to seeing herself on TV with Luke, especially during such a painful exchange. At least she'd missed the episode where she screamed like a raving lunatic. Her new coworkers still razzed her about it.

Her biggest concern was how to sit and watch Luke with Cricket. She liked Cricket, even if she was named after a bug. Luke deserved such a nice woman. It was hard to say if they would last, since most of the reality couples never did, but Cricket was different. She could handle the rich friends, the media, the down-home atmosphere. Ashley wished she could be more like Cricket, but she wasn't.

"Okay fine. I'll watch. But I need more chocolate before you turn on the TV." She paced in front of the counter. "And where's the chocolate ice cream? I'll buy into the whole closure thing, but don't expect me to take it like a man. I plan to get sick as a dog. If I throw up, all for the best. It will be my ceremonial cleansing."

Ashley watched the show, melting chocolate in her hand. At first she was critical of seeing herself on TV. Her nose looked too big and her voice sounded funny. But, after a while, she was transported back to that night, when she had been filled with dread . . . and hope.

As she watched herself walk down the softly lit pathway, she was able to see the experience from a new perspective. On-screen, she actually looked confident and beautiful. She sat on the edge of her seat, transfixed as she observed Luke await her arrival. He was devastatingly handsome. His stance was casual, but she knew how difficult it had been for him too.

Then, as she stepped up to join him, she tripped, and this time he caught and saved her . . . and her pedicure. Ashley smiled, remembering the moment fondly. Kelli sat quietly, watching Ashley.

The rose ceremony continued as Luke gave his beautiful speech to Ashley and released her from the show, and from him. There were no cameras hounding her now, and tears ran freely as she watched them say their final good-bye.

It hurt so much. Still.

Ashley stood during a commercial break to find a tissue to wipe her eyes and nose. It was hard to relive, but it was great to be able to see Luke, to watch his every movement, to watch his expressions change. He exuded quiet strength without even realizing it. Kelli was taping the show, so now she'd have him on tape forever.

Ashley was in the bathroom when Kelli yelled from the other room, "Come on, it's back on."

Not sure if she could watch Luke give the rose to Cricket, she replied, "Okay, in a minute."

When she returned to the living room, Cricket stood in the place she had vacated minutes before. She looked poised and stunning. Ashley watched Luke tell Cricket how much fun he'd had with her and what an extraordinary person she was. They laughed easily as he recalled some of their experiences.

Then the tone changed and Luke became serious. He looked into her eyes and explained how the time on the show had transformed him.

Ashley sat stunned as she heard Luke say, "But after all these weeks, I find myself unable to give my heart." She leaned forward as though the television wasn't loud enough. Had she heard it correctly? Luke continued, "It's not you, or them, but me. I thought I was ready for this step in my life, but I haven't found the fit I was dreaming of. It wouldn't be fair to you to take it any further. So thank you for a wonderful experience. I will never forget our friendship and I wish you great success in life."

He kissed her on the cheek and Cricket graciously said her good-bye, clearly disappointed, but with kindness and understanding on her face.

Ashley couldn't move. She sat with her jaw dropped open.

"He didn't pick Cricket," she whispered in disbelief. "He didn't pick anyone." Her mind reeled as she tried to make sense of what she had witnessed. She turned to Kelli. "He had to pick her. He had to. What happened?"

It didn't make sense. All these weeks, she'd thought he was with Cricket, and now it wasn't the case at all. He'd had to pick her, to keep the producers happy if nothing else. He could have pretended they were dating and then broken it off later.

Bewildered, she turned to Kelli. "You knew?"

Kelli said with caution, "Yes. That's why it was so important you be here tonight to see it for yourself."

Ashley felt dazed and unsure of what to think. They didn't call it a finale for nothing.

Kelli leaned toward her and put her hand on Ashley's. "I realize how difficult this whole ordeal has been for you, and I feel responsible for putting you in such a horrible situation. It never occurred to me that things would go so far or that you would fall for him the way you did."

"Gee, thanks for the vote of confidence."

"You know what I mean. You were there to help me. I never thought ahead to how the show might play out. You didn't do any of the preliminary matching tests. I just assumed, with so many women hand-picked to catch Luke's eye, that you would naturally be released. Anyway, I wanted to make sure you knew the whole story. After the final taping, you disappeared. I understood your need for privacy. You'd fallen for him. But it's important that you be aware of what happened later."

Emotionally exhausted, Ashley leaned back on the couch, staring at the ceiling. "What does this mean?"

"What do you think it means?" Kelli replied.

"I don't know." Ashley shook her head. "I thought he was supposed to pick someone."

"Yes, he was. But he didn't."

Ashley got up and started pacing again. It was so confusing. All this time she'd thought he was with Cricket and loving her. Cricket had fallen for Luke too. It was hard not to.

"I've got to go," she said suddenly, crossing to the front door and reaching for her bag. "I need some time to digest this. I think I'll walk home."

"Are you okay?"

"Yeah, I think so. I just need some air and some time to think it through."

"Will you call me if you need anything?" Kelli looked concerned.

"It's okay. This, too, shall pass." Ashley smiled weakly at her friend and then soundlessly passed through the door, pulling it closed gently behind her.

Ashley took the long way home. It was about a mile and a half. She walked near the lake and took her time. She continued to run the show over and over in her mind. The outcome was a total surprise. Was she happy, or sad, or relieved? Mostly confused. The goal for the evening had been to find closure, to put all the hurt and embarrassment in the past, but closure was the last thing she'd found.

It seemed that Luke felt the same conflicts she did. Before everything fell apart at his parents' house, she would have sworn he cared as much for her as she did for him, but everything had happened so quickly that things were never the same again. She'd lost her cool and her nerve. Her walls had come up and she'd shut him out. She'd made him promise not to give her a rose. So she would never know whether he would have or not. She could dream that he had, but dreams were all they were. This was reality. Not the reality of TV, but of life. They'd shared some beautiful moments together. His impact on her life had made her see a part of herself she hadn't known existed. She loved him like no one she'd ever loved before. And it went both ways. He gave as much as he received. He cared . . . and she had sent him away.

The night grew cooler. She turned away from the lake and made her way back to her apartment. The moon hung heavy in the night sky. It reminded her of their night in Costa Rica.

The raging and volatility were over and now she needed to clean up the debris, put herself back together, and move on. Until the next storm in life blew in.

Ashley climbed the stairs to her apartment. What an emotional night. What an emotional four months! Change was in the air, she was certain. She pulled out her keys and unlocked her door. She set down her purse and tossed the keys onto the side table as she walked in. A strong scent overtook her.

As the lights went on, she saw her apartment was filled with flowers, vases everywhere. Purple delphiniums covered the coffee table, daisies and irises lined the kitchen table, and blue hydrangeas sat massed in pots in front of the TV. There were baskets filled with alstroemeria and stock, with bunches of peonies and lilies in every color. Peach and pink imported orchids surrounded with statice sat in the corners. A huge bunch of lavender was next to the couch. There were lilacs and tulips and little pots overflowing with hyacinths and daffodils. Every place she looked was a different kind of flower, and not just one, but dozens of each. The scent was intoxicating. As she gazed around the room in awe, she caught movement from the corner.

And there he was.

Luke filled the doorway to the kitchen. He leaned casually against the door frame as she took it all in. She was so beautiful, with her hair swinging gently around her face and her graceful movements as she noticed all the flowers.

He watched as her eyes welled up with tears and a smile formed on her lips. Her hand went to her mouth to cover her emotions, but to no avail.

"You're here," she whispered.

He slowly stepped forward. "Yes, I'm here."

"I thought you picked Cricket."

He continued to walk forward. "I know."

"I never thought I'd see you again," she whispered, her voice cracking with emotion.

"I would never let that happen."

He approached her. His body filled her line of vision, tall and strong and confident. He reached down with one hand and pulled a flower from a large bouquet.

"I promised never to give you another rose," he said gazing steadily into her eyes. "So will you accept this flower instead?"

Ashley looked down and saw the purple chicory he held. "It's a weed!" she said, laughing.

"I know, but you said you liked it."

Who but Luke would have remembered and gone to the trouble to gather up a bunch of weeds?

"So, will you accept this flower—I mean, weed?" His eyes twinkled as he offered up the simple bloom. "I can't go another day without you. These past weeks have nearly killed me."

Her eyes filled with disbelief. "You want me?"

"Yes, I want you. That is, if you'll have me. I know I tend to do some really dumb things, so you'll have to be patient," he said. "The truth is I haven't spent a lot of time in love and it seems I mess things up if left to my own devices. Can you possibly forgive me?" He held the chicory like a peace offering.

"Yes, Luke, I can forgive you and I will gladly accept this weed."

He pulled Ashley into his arms, and lowered his mouth to hers. The touch of it warmed his body and filled his soul. She nearly glowed with happiness.

"I'm never going to lose you again, is that clear?" he said sternly looking into her eyes.

"I'd have it no other way," Ashley declared.

"And I will break any camera that ever comes near you again."

"It's okay. Thanks to you, I'm not afraid anymore."